FACSIMILE

VICKI L. WEAVIL

Month9Books

Month9Books

Dedicated to the memory of my father,
John Frederick Lemp, Jr.
1928-2014

A brilliant scientist.
A loving father, husband, grandfather, brother, and friend.
A man respected by all who knew him.
Thanks for everything, Dad.

FACSIMILE

VICKI L. WEAVIL

CHAPTER ONE

A silver form streaks through the azure sky, trailing a flag of flame. The dusting of sand that covers this world of stone swirls around my boots as I climb to my feet.

A ship coming in for a landing.

I run to my solar bike, stuffing two small stones into the pockets of my jeans. The crystals, the color of amethyst, are worthless. But I've traded similar rocks for items of value in the past. Perhaps I'll get lucky again.

Kicking the bike's motor into gear, I speed toward the compound. Wisps of my dark hair whip into my face as I lean over the handlebars. I'm not wearing my helmet, which is worth at least one lecture apiece from my parents and grandparents. But I don't fear a spill, as there's nothing to unseat me. This is Eco—a planet whose landscape consists of large outcroppings

1

of black stone and the occasional twisted tangle of brown vines. Easy enough to spot and avoid.

I spin the bike to a stop just outside the fence that encloses our colony. No large creatures or other dangerous entities roam Eco, so the fence merely marks the boundary between the compound and the rest of the planet. Behind the gates are patches of grass and a few stunted trees—remnants of the terraforming begun by my grandparents and the rest of their crew. The entire planet was to be transformed into a semblance of Earth's most beautiful landscapes, but that was before. Before the NewSkies Corporation went bankrupt and stranded one hundred and thirty terraformers on a planet with breathable air and substantial underground reservoirs of water—but no arable soil.

I slip through the gate and make my way past our small herd of goats. Their paddock is enclosed beneath a dome of porous plastic that allows air in but traps the goats alongside the chickens strutting about the dusty yard. Although we don't worry about predators, we can't afford to lose any of our animals to the wild. They've been carefully bred from their cloned originals, and their milk and eggs are one of the few shields wedged between our colony and starvation.

I lean my bike against the back of the greenhouse that encloses our hydroponic gardens and slap the dust off my thin polysteel jacket, staring over the back gate toward a ribbon of smoothed stone that lies just outside the fence. The beaten-down strip serves as a runway for spacecraft visiting Eco. A pewter-colored ship sits silently on the tarmac, and several figures scramble about its cargo hold.

The back door of the greenhouse flies open. "Anna-Maria." My grandmother's tone is as sharp as her hawk nose. "Where did you gallivant off to? I've been holo'ing you for the last hour."

My grandmother is Paloma Solano, botanist and member of the original terraforming team. She is also one of the few people I fear—and love.

"Sorry. Didn't have my holo turned on." I can read the suspicion in my grandmother's dark eyes. "Did you need my help? I was just going to check out the trader, see if there was anything I could barter … "

"No rush." Grandmother turns her head. Despite the centuries, my grandparents' heritage is unmistakable. Even though e-school history lessons have taught me that Peru is no more, absorbed into the South American Alliance, my grandparents' profiles display the stamp of their Incan ancestors. "Apparently our visitor's having trouble with his environmental controls. This ship will be stuck here while they attempt some repairs."

"Oh, that's too bad." I lift my foot and examine the sole of my boot, using my fingernail to flick out a pebble.

"Plenty of time for you to trade some worthless crystals for credits."

I plant my foot back on the ground and raise my eyes to meet my grandmother's imperious stare. "Is it my fault if people assume things? I never tell them the crystals are actually valuable."

"And you never say they're not. Never mind, nieta—most of these traders deserve to be scammed." Grandmother shields her eyes with one hand as she turns her gaze on the parked spacecraft.

"God knows they cheat us often enough. Now I could use your help for a moment, Anna-Maria."

"Ann." I constantly resist my grandmother's use of my given name. She persists in ignoring me.

She glances at me with raised eyebrows but offers no argument. "Come and assist me with a bit of tubing. You know my fingers don't work as well as they should."

I follow her into the greenhouse, where rows of black bins are shadowed by a canopy of plants suspended from a metal grid. The smell of the nutrient fluid mixed with the odors of the growing plants makes me sniffle. I press my hand against my damp forehead. Although I work here almost every day, I can't adjust to the humidity. I resent the steamy air that drapes over me, heavy as a blanket. It's like a vise—or a trap.

"There." My grandmother points to one of the bins. "I can't seem to grab hold of that feed line properly. Can you pass it up to me?"

I roll back my jacket sleeve. "There's reason number three million four hundred fifty-five thousand why we need to get off this planet. If we were on Earth, we wouldn't have to grow our own food. At least not in a greenhouse. Don't you get sick of it, abuelita, constantly fussing over these plants?"

"Earth's no different." Grandmother's dark eyes rake over me. "You think there's unlimited land left for farming? Most food there is grown hydroponically, just like ours. Where do you think I learned to manage all this?" She sweeps one arm in a circle, indicating the rows of crops.

I dip my hand into the tub and fish around until my fingers

close around the nutrient tube trapped under piece of the drain tray. "I thought the NewSkies Corporation trained you when you signed up to terraform Eco."

"They taught me the science. But I already knew the practicalities. I worked in greenhouses on Earth, you know, when I was younger than you. I had to. No one was handing out credits on the street corner." She takes the freed line from my fingers and threads it through a maze of plastic tubing. "Why do you think we took NewSkies's offer? There was nothing for your grandfather and me on Earth except to work crap jobs and live crammed into some tiny apartment with other members of our family. I've told you this before, nieta, but you tend to tune me out. At least when it involves any stories about Earth that don't paint it as a paradise." Her black eyes narrow as she ties off the tube at just the right angle to feed one tomato plant.

I flip back my heavy braid. Sadly, my brown hair never darkened to match my grandmother's short locks. Although she's over sixty, only a few threads of gray, pale as the meteors that dash across Eco's night sky, streak her black hair. "I don't think Earth is perfect—you and Grandfather constantly remind me of the problems you faced as kids—but it is home. I mean, you were only contracted to stay here for ten years. Then you were going to head back to Earth with a big pile of credits. Say what you want about making the best of things, you gotta admit that you never planned to make Eco your permanent home. If NewSkies hadn't left you stranded, Dad would've been raised on Earth. He wasn't supposed to live here—and I sure wasn't meant to be born here."

My grandmother straightens and stares at me as if seeking

some secret in my eyes. "You might not have been born at all, Anna-Maria, if it weren't for Eco."

"Is that all you needed?" I wipe my hands on my jeans. I have no interest in discussing my parents' less than ideal relationship. Eco may have brought them together, but it's also one of the main reasons they fight. Like me, my mom talks incessantly of leaving our isolated planet, while my dad seems content to stay.

"Yes, I suppose. Run along then. Check out these traders and see what you can pry from their greedy paws. But Anna-Maria," my grandmother fixes me with one of her piercing stares, "don't expect miracles. You know most of these ships can't carry any extra passengers, even if we could afford passage."

I waggle my fingers at her. "I know. See you later!" I dash out of the greenhouse before she can respond.

The public space of the compound is a cluster of metal-clad buildings that lean into each other like drunken revelers. I duck into the recreation hall, tracking my friends by the thump of bass and whine of synthesized guitars. I make my way to the back of the hall—to the game room, its walls papered with wafer-thin holo screens. A jumble of pillows and low gamer chairs, piled high with discarded headpieces and controller gloves, clutter the room. Slouched into one pile of cushions is a boy with hair the color of a sunset sky. Nestled in his pale, freckled arms is my best friend, Emeline Winston.

"Ann." Emie sits up and runs her fingers through her dark curls. "Hear the news?"

"What's that? Hey, Kam."

The boy grunts at me. A real conversationalist, Kameron Frye.

"Well," Emie bats Kam's hand away as he reaches for her waist, "apparently, a member of the ship's crew is our age. The nephew of the captain, or some such thing."

"A seventeen-year-old crew member?" I perch on the edge of a battered table. "That's new."

Emie sits forward and wrinkles her nose. "Yeah, usually it's skuzzy old guys."

"And women," says Kam. He grimaces. "If you can call them that."

Emie's hands rest on Kam's knees. Her warm brown coloring makes his milky skin look anemic by comparison. "Well, most of the younger people are still in the service, I guess. Can't even get a berth unless you've mustered out, and that's years."

"Poor jerks." Kam leans into Emie's back and nips at her ear.

"Oh, and we're better off?" Although there are few people close to our age in the colony, I'm convinced Emie can do better than Kameron Frye. Apprenticed to our colony's computer and communications expert when she was only fourteen, Emie studies every available holodisc, while Kam barely glances at anything educational. I can't imagine what they talk about when alone. Well, to be honest, I suspect a serious lack of conversation in their relationship.

"Hell, yeah," says Kam, unceremoniously sliding Emie off his lap. He stands and stretches, the gap between his shirt and pants exposing a well-muscled expanse of pale skin.

I want to tell him to forget the display, that I have no interest in his torso or any other part of his anatomy, but I bite my tongue. No use upsetting Emie. "Guess that's a matter of opinion."

Emie leans into the cushions, adjusting her position gracefully, as if she'd intended to be dumped to the side. "Well, maybe I'll have to check this guy out. Someone new—could be interesting."

"Calm down, Emie," says Kam. "You don't even know if this dude is a one-hundred-percenter."

"Oh who cares?" Emie slumps back into the cushions.

"You should. Want to end up with some cyber or spacer?"

Emie frowns darkly. "Those Earth laws are crap. We've talked about this before." Her eyes narrow as she glances up at Kam. "Or weren't you listening?"

"Not after the zillionth time you mentioned it." Kam crosses his arms over his chest. "Had to tune it out."

I grimace, praying Kam's remark won't set Emie off. Her meltdown after her research uncovered the truth about Earth's genetic purity laws is legendary. Of course, everyone on Eco has always been aware of the existence of the laws, but our basic educational materials don't dwell on the details. The holodiscs simply mention that the citizens of Earth must carry a file verifying they were born of human parents or risk deportation. Not a problem for me or my family, since everyone on Eco is a "one-hundred-percenter." Our colony isn't home to clones, androids, or others affected by the laws. We occasionally encounter them among the spacer crews that land on Eco, but most colonists avoid prolonged contact with such creatures.

Not Emie. Fueled by her discovery that the laws were enacted primarily to rid the Earth of some of its excess population, she's launched a one-girl crusade to expose the flaws in the regulations. She's particularly incensed by the fact that the laws affect "cybers"—a label slapped on anyone who is over twenty percent cybernetic body parts. Cybers can't be one-hundred-percenters, even though they're born as human as anyone on Earth or Eco.

Kam's green eyes glitter as he stares at Emie. "Whatever. Just be glad we're verified humans. We can live on Earth if we want."

"Not the point." Emie studies Kam with the concentration she usually reserves for her digital circuitry. "When one group is oppressed ... "

"Not that again." Kam grabs his head with both hands and lets out an exaggerated groan. "You'll be granting rights to aliens next."

I'm proud to be a one-hundred-percenter, but Kam's obsession with this subject makes my hands twitch. "Mierda! Emie knows they don't exist."

It's true. After all the stories and films and games, after all our imaginings of aliens, we haven't stumbled over any such beings. Yes, we've discovered some creatures on other planets. But none have matched human sentience. In space, traveling from planet to planet, we are alone. I blink, unsure, as always, why that idea makes my eyes water.

Emie tosses her head. "Anyway, I'm just talking about flirting. A little fun. Not like I plan to have his babies. Got our bioplants to prevent that, thank goodness." She swings one hand, slapping Kam's bare arm. "Or I wouldn't be fooling around with you."

"Yeah, right." Kam grabs her flailing arm and pulls her to his side. He doesn't see the troubled look in Emie's eyes. But I do. Yes, my friend. You can do better.

"Anyway, Ann," Emie tilts her body so there's a hands-width

between her and Kam, "I heard your father invite the captain to dinner. Along with his nephew. So I guess you'll get all the info." There's no disguising the envy in her voice.

I shrug. "Come if you want. I certainly don't give two raps about some guy from a trade ship."

"Well, that's good," says a voice behind me.

I turn to face the speaker. At eighteen, Raiden Lin is six feet of lean, toned muscle and lethal energy. Descended from ancestors who thrived amid the extremes of the Himalayas, his eyes are as dark and silky as his hair, and his smile turns most girls into gibbering fools.

Most girls. I face him down, feet planted apart. "Not that it's any of your business, Raid."

"Isn't it?" Feathery dark brows lift over his black eyes. For a moment I'm distracted by the perfect fringe of his eyelashes and his amused smile. I recall the feel of those lips—that strong, sensual pressure that belies the soft curves of his mouth. Shaking my head, I look away. Everyone on Eco's convinced Raiden Lin and I are destined to marry, or at least to live together. He's just the right age, and we're well matched in intellect and interests. But despite the pleasure I've experienced from his kisses, I'm determined to hold Raid at arm's length. I'm getting off Eco as soon as possible. Somehow I'll find a way to pay for passage on one of the ships that trade their goods for our fresh produce. I don't care if my family and I only take the clothes on our backs, as long as we get back to Earth—back home. I'm willing to leave everything behind.

Except my heart.

"You're such a liar." Raid smoothes back the wisps of damp

hair clinging to my forehead. "Don't know why I waste my time on you, Ann Solano."

"Who else is there?" My tone teases, but I'm deadly serious. Our colony's small by necessity. Our infrastructure can only support a certain number of people, so births are carefully controlled to balance the need for population replacement with resources. Even considering the youngest teens, there are few girls close to Raid's age. It's not as if he has the whole universe to choose from.

"Well, there's Emie." Raid's dark eyes examine my mouth in a way I find entirely too inviting.

"Hey, wait a minute." Kam drops the game controller he's been fondling.

I make a face at Raid. "Emie's spoken for, and you know it. Kam will knock your head off if you make a move on her."

"Damn straight," says Kam.

Raid strokes the line of my jaw with one finger. "Chill, dude. I'm just revving Ann's engines."

"And talking about me like I'm not here," says Emie. "So sweet. Thanks."

I look over at my friend. It's true her boyfriend would likely deck Raid over any flirtation, but I've often wondered if Emie and Raid weren't the better match.

I'll miss her when I leave Eco. The one person I can talk to about anything. But maybe my leaving will benefit her—Raid's certainly a better boyfriend than Kam. Emie will have more options once I've shaken the dust of this rock off my feet. I smother a twinge of jealousy at this thought. I know I like Raid a little too much for my own good, but I can't allow my feelings for him to alter the trajectory of my life. "Anyway, since it seems the parents have invited guests to dinner, I'd better go and clean up."

"Thanks for asking, but I think I'll skip it," says Emie, after a glance at Kam. "We've got plans."

"Plans? On Eco?" I shake my head. "What—a walk under the moons and then a romantic evening playing holo games with all the other people under twenty?"

"No." Emie's dark eyes flash. "Plans. You know. Jeesh, Ann."

"Yes, plans." Raid catches me by the wrist and pulls me close. "The kind of plans we should be making."

I press the heel of my free hand into his breastbone. "You wish." I push him back, twisting my other hand so he's forced to release my wrist. "You people. All you think about is screwing around. Don't you ever want to do anything else, anything more?"

"What the hell else is there?" Kam flops back onto the cushions next to Emie.

I suck in a deep breath. Much as I hate to admit Kam's right about anything, he's spoken the truth. What the hell else is there?

"There has to be something," I reply, talking to myself as much as to the others. "There just has to be." I reach out and take Raid's hand. "Sorry, but I gotta go. Catch you later maybe?"

His eyes are shadowed beneath his dark lashes. "Sure, whatever."

I turn on my heel and leave before he can say anything else. Before the hurt in his eyes can make me pause.

There must be more. Somewhere, far from here, there is something more.

And I will find it once I can find a way to get myself, and my family, off Eco.

CHAPTER TWO

The first thing I notice when I enter our tiny dining and living area is my mother's pink dress.

Mom traded two bins of tomatoes and a holofone for that dress. She only wears it on special occasions. I wouldn't have thought dinner with the captain of a trading ship would merit such attention, but I guess I was wrong.

The pastel dress clings to my mother's curves in a way that draws most men's eyes. Connor Patel, owner and captain of the space trader Augusta Ada, is no exception. His gaze focuses on Mom like a laser, taking in the voluptuous figure that's perfectly proportioned to fit her petite frame. Tara Cooper is the most beautiful woman on Eco—a fact she uses to her advantage whenever possible. Her blond hair, cut short to halo her heart-shaped face, accents her hazel eyes and makes her appear years younger than her actual age.

She's as lovely and delicate as the butterflies I've only seen on holodiscs. But I know all too well the razor-sharp mind lying beneath that golden cap of hair. Those who underestimate my mother do so at their peril.

I've never dared. My father's genes may have dominated my appearance, but my intelligence is an inheritance from both parents

"Hello," I say, glancing about. I notice my father is seated near my grandparents, across the table from my mom. My eyes come to rest on the young man seated next to Captain Patel. The boy is a slighter, paler facsimile of the older man, with the same dark hair and the same liquid brown eyes fringed with impossibly thick black lashes.

"Ann." My mother motions for me to sit across from the young man. "Everyone, this is our daughter, Anna-Maria. Though she prefers you call her Ann."

My grandmother coughs to cover some comment in Spanish. I tap my grandfather's shoulder as I sit between him and my father. We share a conspiratorial glance over my grandmother's not-so-subtle reaction.

"So," says Captain Patel, "I assume you were two of the first people on Eco, Paloma and … ?"

"Zolin." My grandfather's lips tighten. He's clearly irritated the captain has already forgotten his name. "Paloma and Zolin Solano. Our son, Jason, is your host. Along with Tara, of course."

"And such gracious hosts too." Patel lifts his glass. I note it's filled with the wine Grandfather distills from grapes grown on

Grandmother's hydroponic vines. Also something reserved for special occasions.

My mother seats herself beside Captain Patel, and I allow my gaze to wander about the room, wondering how our home appears to our visitors. Probably much like the quarters on their ship. Our small living space, with its riveted metal walls and tiny windows, closely resembles the interior of a spacecraft.

"Ann," my mother holds her glass between her thumb and forefinger like the stem of a rose, "this is Captain Connor Patel and his nephew, Dacian Keeling."

"Dace," says the young man. His full lower lip rolls into a pout.

I smile at him. It seems he also struggles with name difficulties. "Dace—that's cool. Never known anybody with that name before. Captain Patel," I nod my head. I've already heard his name bantered about the colony gossip mill, but it's probably best not to acknowledge it.

"Dacian's a scientist," the captain says. "I brought him along on this trip primarily for his own good. He's conducted research and exploration on each of the planets we've visited."

"A modern-day Darwin?" My father leans forward to pass a platter of roasted vegetables to our guests. "Sorry, there's no meat. Not very practical here, you understand."

Patel's short black hair gleams with blue highlights under our solar lamps. "Quite all right. I've been a vegetarian all my life."

"My uncle grew up in India," says Dace, spooning a heaping pile of vegetables onto his plate. "With my mom, who still lives there. I was born there too," he adds, between bites.

So Dace passes the one-hundred-percenter test. I'll have to tell Emie.

"Does that mean Dacian's mother is your sister?" Mom taps Patel's arm with her slender fingers. "There's some goat cheese there, to your right, if you eat dairy."

"Yes, sister. Our parents have passed, so it's just Nadia and me and Dacian."

"What about your dad?" My father asks, directing his words at Dace. "What does he do?"

The boy stabs a carrot with his fork. "Disappears."

"You have cattle?" Patel asks, reaching for the plate of cheese.

"Goats," says my grandmother. "Brought the cloned genetic material with us and grew our own. Cows are too difficult." She shrugs. "Too large, too particular about what they eat."

"You still clone copies?" Dace's eyes brighten with interest.

"No, we let nature take its course now. Easier." My grandmother spoons roasted sweet potatoes, carrots, and endive onto her plate. "But we preserve some of the original genetic material, of course. One never knows what will happen. Best to be prepared."

"Chickens too," I say brightly, then stare at the vegetables on my plate. Stupid comment. Typical. When I get excited I tend to jabber.

"Really?" Dace's tone makes me lift my head and look at him. "But you don't let them mingle with the native animals, do you?"

Grandfather snorts. "Aren't any. Well, none of any consequence. Insects of some kind, a few lizard-like things. Nothing else we've ever found. Doubt Eco will offer you much to study, Dace." He takes the vegetable platter from my grandmother and sets it on the table. "But no, we don't let our livestock mingle with the native environment. That's why we have the domes."

"Yeah, I saw those." Dace taps his fork against his plate. "I'd like to go out and take a look, though, all the same." His eyes meet mine. He does have beautiful eyes. I can just imagine Emie's reaction. Perhaps I'd better warn Dace about Kam's territorial nature.

"As a matter of fact, I have a proposition for you—well, for anyone in your colony who might be interested." Patel leans back in his chair, flexing his muscled arms.

"Oh, and what might that be?" My mother stirs the food around on her plate. In my head I urge her to eat, but I know she'll only take a few bites.

"Well, I obviously need a few parts to repair my ship. Thought you might have something lying about that I could use. I'm willing to barter some of my cargo—and I also need a favor."

Grandmother eyes the captain with what I've always termed her interrogator look. "What kind of favor?"

"Nothing extreme, or illegal." Patel turns to my mother on those last words and grins with very white teeth.

My mother smiles in return. "Well, that doesn't sound like much fun."

I peek at Dace from under my lowered eyelids. He's shoveling food into his mouth, studiously ignoring the adults.

"Just what is this favor?" my father asks, as he chops his vegetables into tiny pieces.

"I need someone familiar with Eco to escort Dacian around

the planet. Not the whole place, of course. I know that's impossible. But show him around the nearby area and keep him safe while he conducts a bit of research."

"And what are you willing to exchange for this favor?" Dad lays down his knife. "It could be dangerous, you know. We don't like anyone wandering too far afield. Things happen."

He glances at my mother, whose smile has evaporated. Mom's parents were geologists who died before I was born. Also a geologist, Mom rarely uses her training, preferring to solve disputes as part of the colony's governing council.

"I could make it worth someone's while," says Patel, scooping up the last remnants of sweet potato with a piece of flatbread.

"How so?" My mother toys with her silver bracelet. I remember when Dad traded a fan motor off one of the abandoned terraforming machines for that piece of jewelry. It was a gift for one of their anniversaries.

"At the end of the run. Headed back to Earth once we get repairs made. Have a bit of room on the ship, and enough provisions with some of your produce loaded onto the Ada. Could take a few people back with us." He glances around the room, his eyes taking in our bleak, cramped living quarters. "If anyone's interested."

I catch his eye and stare into his strong-featured face. Perhaps he can read the naked desire in my eyes. Perhaps everyone can. "How many people?"

"Oh, four or five."

"And you just need someone to act as a guide for Dace?" I catch a glimpse of my grandfather's disapproving gaze.

"That's it. Of course, I want to offer this opportunity to the entire colony, you understand. But I'm thinking perhaps a young person would be best. Someone around Dacian's age."

Dace looks up from his plate and stares at his uncle. The pout is back.

"That'd be perfect," I say, as my father's foot presses over mine. "I can tell the other kids tonight."

"Would you?" Patel turns to my mother, his eyes alight. "What a charming daughter you have, Ms. Cooper. So helpful."

"Yes, isn't she?" My grandmother shoots me a fierce look.

Mom pushes back her half-empty plate and stretches languidly. "Ann is quite clever. Pity her talents will be wasted here on Eco."

"Now, Tara, let's not start that." Dad wipes his mouth on one of our carefully hoarded cloth napkins.

"Not many options for a girl with brains and ambition around here." My mother looks over at Connor Patel. "It's really a shame. We work to survive, you know. Subsistence living, they call it. I call it a pity, especially for a girl who wants much more from life than mere survival."

Patel's gaze is fixed on my mother's face, which glows pink as a sunrise. My grandfather coughs loudly.

"No one's talents need be wasted if they're employed in good, hard work." Grandmother stands, throwing her napkin across her empty plate. "If you'll excuse me, I have some fruit grafts that need my attention."

"At this hour?" asks my father. One look from Grandmother and he falls silent.

"Anna-Maria, if you're finished eating, perhaps you could assist me?"

"Bien. But if Mom needs me to clean up?"

My mother waves her hand in dismissal. Her bracelet jingles as it slides down her slender arm. "Thank you, dear, but your father will help me. Run along."

I glance at Dace as I push back my chair and rise to my feet. He returns my look with a stare that examines me as if I were one of his specimens. "Nice to meet you." I bob my head at the two men before following my grandmother out of the room and into the hall that runs between the rows of family quarters.

"How long do you think we'll be?" I ask Grandmother's rapidly retreating back. "I said I'd tell the other kids. They're probably in the rec hall. I can catch them all at once."

"Niña tonta—I don't actually need your help. Just wanted to get out of there," she calls over her shoulder.

"So why'd you ask me to come along? I could've talked to Dace some more."

Reaching the door that leads outside, my grandmother turns to me. Her face is shadowed in the dim light of the hall. "Ann-Maria Solano, I know what you're up to. I know how desperately you want to leave Eco. But listen to me carefully, nieta—just getting our family to Earth won't do it."

"Won't do what?"

"Make her love him."

I stare at my grandmother for a moment. Shoving open the door, I stride past her and into the cool, dark night.

CHAPTER THREE

As I make my way toward the recreation hall, I consider my grandmother's warning. She thinks she knows better than me, but in this case she's wrong. I've heard my parents fight often enough to know it's my mother's hatred of Eco that fires their arguments. Grandmother should know that too, since she lives with us, but I think she's just in denial. Like my dad, she isn't really interested in leaving Eco.

But I'm convinced Earth, with all its problems, has to be better than here, where nothing ever happens and nothing changes. No wonder it drives my mother nuts. If we were all living on Earth, where there are new people, fresh opportunities ...

I hear footsteps and spy a shadow starting to spread around me. I spin about and come face to face with Dacian Keeling.

"Sorry. My uncle was being a bit of a jerk."

I flip my braid over my shoulder. "Not really."

"Yeah, he was. Checking out your mother and all." Dace shrugs. "He does that sort of stuff all the time. It doesn't really mean anything."

"I didn't think ... " I observe the unfettered honesty in Dace's eyes and shut my mouth.

"You did. It was pretty obvious. But don't worry—Connor won't do anything stupid. He's a pretty good guy, really."

"He must be. Bringing you along just so you can be a researcher, or whatever."

"Naturalist, actually." Dace scuffs the tip of his boot against the hard ground. "It's mostly rock, the surface?"

"Mostly." I examine his narrow face, bleached to beige under the solar-powered outdoor lights. "How come you're not in school, then? University, I mean. Don't you need a degree to be a real scientist?"

"Well, duh." Dace studies me for a moment. "Sorry, you probably don't know how difficult it is these days."

"To go to college? Why? Most everything's digital. I mean, our access to the 'sphere is kind of spotty sometimes, but even I can trade with spacers for educational holodiscs." I lean against one wall of the dairy, which backs up onto the rec building.

"No, I mean it's hard to get in—officially. Sure, you can take classes through the 'sphere and holodiscs and all, but to get a real degree, something that matters, you have to be accepted into an actual university. And that's almost impossible, unless ... "

"You're rich?"

"Yeah, or your family has the right status. Most of the spots get passed down, parents to kids, or whatever." Dace hugs his arms to his chest. "My family isn't wealthy, and we sure as hell aren't important. So the only way I can grab a spot is if I present some pretty spectacular research and snag one of the few scholarships."

"Oh, that's why you're traveling with your uncle? Smart." I examine him more closely. "Cold? Should've warned you—nights on Eco can get chilly. Come on, let's pop inside." I motion toward the dairy.

"It isn't locked?" asks Dace.

I flip the latch and push the door open. "Locked? What's there to steal? And where would anyone take it?" I lead him into the dark confines of the pasteurization room. "Steal something on Eco and everyone will know it's gone in twenty minutes—and figure out who took it in thirty."

"That's so weird." Dace perches on one of the empty metal milk cans. "Where I grew up, nobody could keep track of anyone else's business. Way too many people." He glances around, taking in the gleaming vats and metal tubing. "How'd you get all this stuff, anyway? I thought your grandparents and the others were just dumped here."

"No," I say, sitting on the milk can next to him. "NewSkies had the infrastructure for the colony set up before they sent anyone to live here. And for the first few years they supplied everything needed. After that," I sweep back the hair that's sprung free from my braid, "well, the colonists had to make do. They stripped some of the terraforming equipment for parts. Now we keep everything going by being very careful and immediately repairing anything that breaks. And trading, of course."

"You barter produce for stuff from passing ships?"

"Pretty much. Sometimes we even let go of old equipment parts, but only if we don't see any future use for them. And we do have a couple 3-D copiers to replicate certain parts, if we can scrounge enough scrap metal or plastic."

Dace searches my face, his pupils very wide as he peers through the darkness. "Why didn't you leave? I mean, why didn't your grandparents leave the planet when they got abandoned? Why stay here?"

"They couldn't." I turn my head away. "Their transport ships were designed to be dismantled to build their living quarters. After that ... well, we don't exactly have access to piles of credits here, and vegetables or a few spare parts won't pay for passage on any spacecraft."

"So, trapped, basically."

"Basically."

"That sucks."

"It does. Listen, Dace." When I lay my hand on his wrist he jerks his arm away. Weird. I'm used to guys welcoming any physical contact. "I was wondering if you could convince your uncle to choose me as your escort. I know this planet as well as anyone, and actually ... " My mind races for anything I can use as bait, since flirtation obviously won't work. "Actually, you'd get to explore a lot more if I'm your guide. I'd be willing to take you to places no one else will go. The rock hills, for example. You know, those outcroppings? Most people on Eco won't take you near them."

"Why not?" I can tell by his tone Dace is intrigued.

"They're pretty unstable. Rock slides and all." A holo image of the grandparents I never knew flits through my mind. "But I'm not worried about stuff like that. I know how to study them without danger."

This is a lie. I know nothing about the rock hills and have never dared to explore them. But by the time we reach that point in our tour, I'm sure I can come up with some excuse to avoid those rock piles.

"I'll see what I can do." Dace gets back on his feet, vigorously rubbing his arms with his hands. "Listen, I'd better go back. My uncle will wonder where I've gone, and I don't want to worry him." He tilts his head to the side and looks me over once more. "You'll really take me places the others won't?"

I hop off my makeshift seat. Straightening to my full height, I look Dace dead in the eye. "I can, and I will."

"Good." Dace's teeth gleam in the darkness.

His smile changes his face. He's almost handsome. I shake my head. No use thinking that way. I have enough problems dealing with Raid.

"See you later then," I say, heading for the door. "Can you find your way back okay?"

"Sure. Not such a big place, is it?" Dace crosses in front of me to walk out of the building. Halfway across the yard, he pauses. "I'll put in a word for you with Uncle Connor. Promise." He turns and jogs toward our living quarters.

I wait until he safely enters that building before leaving the dairy and heading into the recreation hall.

Of course, I have to share Patel's offer with the others. Word gets around the compound so fast, there's no way I can keep it a secret. But I also need to make sure no one else is interested.

The game room's filled with young people. Most are playing Deep Sea Survival. The game's visuals swirl around me, making me feel as if I'm sinking through a shark-infested ocean trench. I squint to avoid getting caught up in the holographic images.

"Well, look who's here." Emie sidles up to me and slips her arm through mine. "I thought you'd still be hanging out with the spacers."

"No, it was just dinner. Hey," I shout over the booming sound system, "can you mute that thing? I've got a message."

Kam rises from a battered couch, waving his gloved hand. The game instantly pauses. "What's up?"

Several pairs of eyes fix on me. I know everyone, of course, though most are not what I'd call friends. The majority of people in the room are younger than me by at least three years. Raid, Emie, Kam, and I are four of the six people between the ages of sixteen and eighteen in the colony. Raid always jokes there must've been a three-year ban on sex after we were conceived.

"Are you babysitting?" I raise my eyebrows at Emie. "Thought you had other plans for tonight."

"That's later," she replies, motioning with her head toward the tumble of kids occupying cushions tossed on the floor. I spy her sister, Lily, and Kam's cousin, Trent. "Raid's snagging some snacks from the storeroom, if you're looking for him."

"No, not right now. I just need to deliver a message." I wave my hands. "Hey, guys, listen up. I know not everyone's here, but you can pass this along to your families and friends, okay?"

"Sure, whatever," says Trent, fiddling with his game controller glove. He has Kam's pale coloring, offset by dark hair and vivid blue eyes. If he were a bit older than fourteen, Emie would probably consider throwing Kam over for his gorgeous cousin.

"The captain of the Augusta Ada, the trading ship that landed today, has made an offer." When I explain Patel's bargain, several faces light up. I'm not the only one with dreams of leaving Eco. "The bad thing is … " As I pause for effect, Raid enters the room, toting a canvas bag.

"Snacks, you monsters." Before he tosses the bag to Kam, he pulls out a precious bar of chocolate. Someone must've traded a bin of produce for that. "Here." He presses the candy into my hands. "Don't say I never gave you anything."

I tap the bar against my palm. "I was just telling everyone about an opportunity." I summarize Patel's offer as I peel the paper from the chocolate then wave the bar under Raid's nose. "But, the thing is—I think the captain's lying."

"Why's that?" Emie moves close to Kam, who wraps his arm around her waist. She allows the embrace, but doesn't lean into him.

"Yeah, what's the deal?" Raid asks, leaning in to take a bite of the chocolate. His eyes meet mine as he straightens. Eyes as dark as the chocolate and just as tempting.

"I overheard him when he didn't know I was around. Near the ship, with one of his crew, right before I came in here." I lie without hesitation, my gaze fixed on Raid's face.

The other young people in the room all focus on me. This had better be good. "He said he was just conning us. He does want someone to escort his nephew about the planet, but he has no intention of taking anyone with him when he leaves." I shrug. "Don't know what excuse he'll use, or if he'll just lift off without telling anyone, but I don't think he plans to keep his word."

"So, we shouldn't bother?" Trent's blue eyes mist with tears. He looks away, nonchalantly brushing at his face with his sleeve. No, I'm not the only one desperate to leave Eco. Trent has a fascination with science that holodiscs and intermittent access to the 'sphere can't satisfy.

"Well, that's up to you. I thought maybe I'd show the kid around, just to be polite. But don't expect any favors from Captain Patel." I break off a piece of the chocolate and pop it in my mouth.

Without warning, Raid leans in and kisses me. "Mmmm, tasty," he says, as he pulls away.

"Gross, Raid." I wipe my mouth with the heel of my hand.

"Really?" He steps back, his face blank as a mask. "Way to kill a mood, Ann."

"Like sticking your tongue in my mouth when I'm not expecting it?"

"Some girls would like that." Raid tugs up his pants, which have slipped down his narrow hips.

"You need a belt. Or smaller pants," I say, shoving the rest of the chocolate into my mouth. I know I'm being cruel, and I don't care. I can't have Raiden Lin seducing me into staying on Eco. Not when I'm so close to leaving.

Raid stares at me for a moment before shaking his head. "What a baby." He turns to Emie and Kam. "Isn't she a baby?"

"Now, Raid," says Emie.

"Yes," says Kam.

"So why don't you run along, little girl? Back to your mommy and daddy." Raid's black eyes flash. "I'm sure they can show you how to behave like a grown-up. Oh wait, maybe not."

I step forward and slap Raid hard across the face. All heads in the room swivel to look at us. I stand motionless, cradling one hand with the other. "Sorry," I mutter. But I'm not sure this is true.

Emie rushes forward. "Kam, turn the game back on," she orders, as she steps between Raid and me. "You two settle down. Don't air your crap in public."

"Sorry," I say again, as holographic images spring to life all around me. I stare into the dead eyes of a shark as it swims near my face. "But really, Raid, you didn't have to be so freakin' rude."

"I apologize," he says. "Shouldn't bring the parents into it. But the smack-down might have been overkill."

"I just … I don't know." I blow at the imaginary shark and it turns and glides away.

"You never know, Ann." There's a sadness in Raid's voice that makes me wince.

I lay my fingers over one of his rigid arms. "You just want more than I can give right now. We've talked about this before."

"Yeah." Raid lifts his other arm and brushes his thick black hair away from his forehead. "We've talked and talked. Well, I'm done, Ann." He shakes off my hand. "Come and find me when you're ready to do more than talk." Turning on his heel, he strides out of the game room.

"He'll be back," says Emie, pulling me in for a hug.

I hear the outer door of the recreation building slam.

It doesn't matter. I'll be gone soon. Far away. It's really better for Raid if he isn't that attached when I leave.

It really is better.

"Come on," I say to Emie. "I bet I can survive longer than you—or Kam," I add, with a glance at her boyfriend.

"Fat chance." Kam throws me a controller glove. "Prepare to be humbled, Solano."

Emie gives my arm a pat before backing away. "Give me one of those too, Kam. I'll help Ann."

Kam grins and tosses her a glove. "I'll take on the two of you. Easy win."

Emie and I look at each other.

"Let's wipe the ocean floor with him," I say.

"Oh, let's." Emie smiles as we flop onto the couch on either side of Kam.

I turn off the part of my mind whispering stupid, painful things—things about Raid and how he makes me feel like my stomach's filled with trapped moths—and concentrate on the game. Tomorrow I'll escort Captain Patel's nephew around Eco, and after that, who knows? Perhaps I'll finally be jetting to Earth, where I belong.

Where there are endless opportunities and millions of young men with dark eyes.

CHAPTER FOUR

Gently wrapping fabric tape, I hear the greenhouse door open and close. I don't look up until I finish the delicate process of grafting a slip of standard apple tree onto dwarf stock.

"Your dad said you'd be here." Dace faces me across the workbench. "I wanted to let you know my uncle's made his choice."

I push the pot holding the grafted sapling to one side. "And?"

Dace examines the tree with interest. "Is this what you do? When you're not studying holodiscs or hanging out, I mean?"

"Yes, I'm apprenticed to my grandmother. Now—what did he decide?"

"He said you could show me around. Seems like no one else was eager to volunteer, even with his offer." Dace studies me with a question in his eyes. "You *did* carry the message to the others?"

"I did." I wipe my hands on my jeans. One way to disguise

the trembling in my fingers.

"Anyway, no one stepped forward. I thought it was weird that not a single person was interested." Dace is still staring at me. "Except for you, of course. So I guess you're it."

I cough to cover the laugh threatening to erupt from my throat. "Bien. When do you want to start?"

"Today? Is that possible?"

"Sure." I sweep up my grafting tools and slip them into the workbench drawer. "But you need to do some prep. First of all, you need an emergency kit." I list off the items Dace must carry with him whenever he travels beyond the compound.

Dace scribbles the list into his holofone. "Is it that dangerous?"

"Not if you're prepared." I look him over, noting his loose cotton T-shirt and pants. "You'll need to wear jeans. Jeans and a polysteel jacket. And boots. Ground's hard and rocky. No place for soft shoes."

Chewing on his stylus, Dace stares at the screen of his fone. "I don't have the jacket. Not much use for one on the ship, and the other planets we've visited required more protection."

"Oh, space suits or something? That must've been awkward."

"Hard to work in at first, but you get used to it." Dace taps the stylus against his chin. "You're lucky Eco has an Earth-like atmosphere. Makes everything so much easier."

I frown. Dace might think we're fortunate, but he doesn't know what it's like to actually live here. "Yes, well ... Eco has its own problems. No surface water. That was the major focus of the terraforming. They were planning to bring the underground water to the surface."

"I know. I read that." Dace smiles, displaying teeth as white and even as his uncle's. "Looked it up last night in your holo library."

"Well, aren't you the researcher." I move toward the exit. "Come on; let's get your emergency kit together. And find you a jacket." Pausing at the doors, I look him up and down. "One of mine might fit you. You're skinny enough. Should work. Unless you're funny about wearing a girl's jacket."

"I don't care." Dace steps closer until we're toe to toe. "Who's going to see us?"

We're about the same height—he only has an inch on me. Accustomed as I am to Raid's height and larger frame, it seems strange to be standing so close to a boy just barely bigger than me. But it isn't a bad feeling. With Dace, I feel like I'm the one who's older, who's the protector. Which I might have to be if we encounter any problems out in the wilderness.

"Follow me," I say, and am secretly pleased when he does.

As we cross the barren yard that lies between the greenhouse and the living quarters, Raid and Kam stroll out of the recreation hall.

"Well, if it isn't Solano and the little scientist," says Kam.

Raid crosses his arms against his chest and glowers.

"Thought you two would be working." I meet Raid's stare with a glare of my own.

"Got the day off," Raid says. Since he works with my grandfather, I suspect this is a lie. Grandfather never takes a day off during the week, and I know he demands Raid follow his example. He claims it will take Raid a few more years to master the intricacies of the 3-D copiers used to replicate certain machine parts and small household goods.

"And you never work if you can help it," I say to Kam.

The redhead motions upward, toward the tall windmills spinning in the steady breeze. "No need. Turbines working just fine. Anyway, it's none of your biz, Solano."

"So all your energy comes from wind and solar?" Dace's tone conveys a serious interest in the answer.

I glance at him, impressed that he displays no signs of being intimidated. "Yes. That's why it's important," I make a face at Kam, "that the energy jockeys responsible for the collectors don't crap out on their jobs."

Kam snorts. "Like you're always slaving away in the greenhouse? Nobody buys that, Solano."

"Now Kam, be fair." Raid's dark eyes are fixed on me with a gaze that makes heat rise in my face. "Ann takes her work seriously. Just not anything else."

Dace looks from Raid to me and back again. "Right now," he says, his voice devoid of emotion, "Ann's going to be my guide while I do some research on your planet's plants and animals."

"Oh? So she can take your uncle's offer to jet off Eco, I suppose?" Raid drops his arms to his sides, but his fists remain clenched.

"That's the idea," says Dace. "So if you don't mind, we need to go and get stuff together for our first expedition. I don't want to waste any time. Not sure when the ship will be repaired, and I know Connor won't want to hang around here any longer than necessary."

Raid's eyes narrow. "Is that right, Ann? You'll be leaving us soon?"

"Could be," I reply, giving him a warning look. As Dace glances back at the windmills, I mouth, "He doesn't know," at Raid.

Raid's black eyebrows rise to meet the swoop of black hair falling across his brow. "Interesting. Well, let's hit the kitchens, Kam, and see what we can scrounge for breakfast."

I shake my head. "You haven't eaten yet?"

"Just got up. Late night." Raid shoots me a significant look.

This might bother me if I thought there was another girl, but I know all about his limited choices. One of the many reasons I can't take his desire for me too seriously. Who else is he going to pursue? Emie is off-limits, and his other options are Karla, who'd be uninterested even if she wasn't already in a relationship with Caroline, and the fifteen and unders. It's me by default. Somehow, being the only option doesn't thrill me.

Raid pulls an exaggerated yawn. "Yeah, didn't get much sleep. How 'bout you, Kam?"

"Me neither. Or Emie." Kam gives me a wink.

Of course, there are the older women in the colony, but they're all matched with someone. Although, as I study Raid's face—with its heavy-lidded eyes and self-satisfied smile—I wonder.

"Well, I certainly don't want to keep you from … food." I lift my chin and refuse to look away from Raid's intense gaze. "Dace and I will just get our stuff together and head out while you guys chow down."

"See ya later, losers," says Kam. "Come on, Raid. Let the kiddies go exploring."

"Sure." Raid flashes one of those smiles that always catch me off-guard. "Have fun, Ann. I'm sure it'll be a blast." He nods his head toward Dace. "Beautiful scenery, stimulating company, and all that."

Dace turns to me, his expression clearly indicating confusion. "I'm sure Ann will be a great guide."

"Hell yes." Raid leans in and pats Dace on the shoulder. "She'll be terrific. She's got the proper scientific mindset. Detached and analytical—that's her."

Kam laughs. "You should see your face, Solano."

"Hijo de puta," I mutter, before turning to Dace. "Don't worry about them. They have nothing better to do than tease. Makes them feel superior, I guess."

As I turn to leave, Raid grabs my arm. "Be careful out there," he says in a very different tone of voice. "Remember what happened to your grandparents."

I look back at him. "I'm always careful." Shaking off Raid's hand, I stalk away, not bothering to check if Dace is following.

"What was that all about?" Dace jogs to my side, matching his pace to my furious strides.

"Oh, nothing." I glance at him. His face displays concern rather than any prurient interest. "Nothing to worry about. Living on Eco—it's just like some tiny town in those classic holo books. Everybody knows everyone else and watches everything you do … Sometimes it gets on your nerves, you know?"

"I see the problem," says Dace thoughtfully. "It's not like you can meet new people any day of the week."

"No, we don't have many choices in our friends, or anything

else." I pause at the entrance to the living quarters. "Head to your ship to change and gather those things I suggested, and meet me back here as soon as possible. I'm going to grab bikes, my kit, and some jackets, but that'll only take a sec." I study him for a moment. "What's wrong?"

"Nothing. Just don't want to waste your time if you have better things to do."

I snort. "Better things? On Eco? Hardly. Anyway, it'll be cool to see what you do. For your research, I mean. And you'll get some good samples, I promise."

"Great." Dace smiles. The expression lights up his narrow face.

I can't help but smile in response. "So—back here in a few. Then off we go, trekking into the unknown like those ancient explorers."

"Making great discoveries," says Dace. "Hey, don't smirk—you never know. It's always possible."

"Anything's possible," I say, and for the first time in many years, I believe it.

CHAPTER FIVE

D ace has no trouble handling the solar bike, zooming ahead and even spinning a few wheelies as we speed over the flat terrain.

"You've done this before," I yell at him over the hum of the electric engines.

He just grins at me from behind his helmet visor before zipping away.

I gun my engine to keep up with him. I'm not comfortable with the speed we're traveling, but I refuse to allow this tourist to best me.

"There might be hidden rocks, moron!" I shout. "Keep your eyes open!"

He nods, but I have the feeling he's laughing at me.

Close to the first of the black rock outcroppings, I swing my bike around in a wide arc in front of him.

Dace slows his bike to a normal speed.

"Stop here." I gesture toward the rocks. "Best place to start looking for stuff." I kill my engine and climb off my bike.

Dace stops and pulls off his helmet before dismounting. I giggle. His dark hair is standing up all around his head, framing his face like spikes.

"That bad?" He runs his hands through his hair, succeeding only in flattening it slightly. "So, what should I be looking for?"

"I don't know. You're the scientist." I slide off my own helmet, thankful my tight braid has kept my hair relatively neat. "There're a few insect thingies that hang out around these rocks, and some lizard-type creatures. Thought you might be interested."

"Come out here often?" Dace pulls a small pouch from one of his bike bags.

"Sometimes. There are these crystals I collect for barter. Not especially valuable, but pretty. Look like amethysts. Traders seem to like them."

Unwrapping some digital gadgets and small metal tools, Dace glances up at me with a little smile. "Crystals, huh. Do you tell these traders what they're really worth?"

"Not always," I admit. "I mean, I don't state they're actually valuable."

"And you don't say they're not."

"Merida! You sound like my grandmother."

Dace's eyes spark with humor. "Not what I was going for." He examines one of his gadgets. "So, this Raid guy. Is he your boyfriend?"

"Uhm, no. Well, maybe." I rub at the side of my nose. "Guess it depends on what you call a boyfriend."

"Dating? Kissing? Stuff like that." Dace walks toward the cluster of black rocks, holding up some type of digital device.

"We hang out sometimes," I say, not sure why I don't want to admit to anything more. "What about you? Did you leave some girl pining for you back on Earth?"

"Nah. Never had time." Dace waves the device around then pulls it back and peers into the screen.

"Time was really a problem?" I watch Dace with interest, wondering what he's measuring.

Dace glances at me with a rueful smile. "Okay, so it wasn't only time. I just never met anyone who interested me that much. I mean, enough to want to spend a lot of time with them. And to be honest, I didn't seem to fascinate the girls that much. I'm not, you know, really built or anything."

"I don't think that's the main … " Dace holds up his hand and I snap my mouth shut.

"Got it!" In front of him a small circle of light glimmers. Within that faintly illuminated globe darts a flying insect. "Don't worry, it won't be harmed."

"I'm not worried. Those things pester me to death when I'm outside. Kill it, for all I care."

"I don't want to kill anything," says Dace with a frown. "Have you ever really taken a good look at these creatures? They're pretty awesome."

I move closer and stare into the sphere. The insect has the gossamer wings of a dragonfly, but its body resembles something else. "Looks like those seahorses from Earth. Pictures I've seen, anyway."

"Yeah, it has the biological structure of a sea creature. Weird, considering the lack of oceans here." Dace swipes a finger across his digital device and the globe disintegrates. The winged creature flies away.

"I thought you wanted to gather samples."

Dace taps the device with his forefinger. "I have it in here. This can analyze any living creature and download all its vital information without harm. All the info I need is stored for later study."

"Wow—must've cost a fortune."

Dace shrugs. "I worked several part-time jobs to buy my equipment. Saved up for a while."

I sit on one of the rocks that have tumbled off the larger pile. "Didn't you go to school? I mean, I know we just study independently here on Eco, but I thought it was different on Earth."

"It is different—if you're rich." Dace squats down and examines the base of the rock pile. "My family couldn't afford for me to go to school. So I did the holodisc and 'sphere thing, just like you. At least that was free, thanks to the library. Hey, did you know there's air rising up from under these rocks?" He places his hand over one of the small fissures in the pile.

"What's that mean?"

"Probably caverns under here. Makes sense. You said there's lots of underground water?"

"Yes, but near the compound it's held in pockets. Natural cisterns."

Dace holds up his hand, palm up. "Damp. Which means there's water down there. I bet that's where those flying insect-like creatures actually live." He leans forward and peers at the base of the rock pile.

"Careful. Those stones are unstable." I shift on my hard seat. I certainly don't want to lose my family's ticket off Eco to a slide.

"Damn!" Dace rocks back on his heels. He swings his electronic device in a wide arc over the ground and another globe forms.

Trapped in its soft glow is a tiny lizard-like creature.

"Oh, wow." Dace gets down on his hands and knees to stare into the globe. "Come look at this, Ann."

I don't move. "I've seen them skittering around plenty of times."

"Yes, but have you ever really looked at them? I mean, really looked." Dace turns his head to gaze at me.

The wonderment in his eyes captures my attention. I slide off the rock and crawl over to examine the creature. "What's so fascinating?"

"Well, check it out." Dace sits up, making room for me to peer into the globe.

At first glance, it looks like an ordinary lizard. At least, like all the holo images of lizards I've seen. As I look closer, I realize the creature is covered in perfect, iridescent scales. Its tiny head has the snout of alligator, but its eyes, quite large for its face, are as green as new leaves.

"It's beautiful." I whisper, surprised to hear those words leave my mouth.

"Yes, and again, more like something that lives mostly in water, not on land." Dace adjusts something on the device then swipes to free the little creature. It darts away, disappearing into a small crack in the rock pile.

"Well, you've lucked out so far. Those two things are basically all I've ever seen around here." I rise to my feet, brushing the sand from my jeans. "There's one other little insect thing. Smaller than the one you found. Don't know if we'll see any of those today, though. They usually come out closer to dusk."

"This is fantastic." Dace stands, slipping the digital device into his pocket. "Really." He turns to me with a bright smile. "Thank you, Ann. You knew exactly where to look."

"But not how, apparently." I am still processing my reactions to the two creatures we've found. Though I've seen them so many times, until Dace pointed them out I never really looked at them. I never realized they were so unique or beautiful.

"Most people don't," says Dace, without rancor. "Everyone just moves along lost in their own heads, never noticing much."

"Except you."

"Well, I'm a naturalist. Comes with the territory. And I like to see things, you know, the way they really are. Not just what I think they might be." Dace steps back and stares at the pile of large rocks. "Did you ever study the Impressionists?"

"The artists? Sure. Pretty cool stuff."

"Well, that was their thing, looking at landscapes and objects and even people with a clear eye. Really seeing, without filtering through the lens of what they expected to see." Dace reaches out and slips his fingers between two of the rocks. "Looking without prejudice or preconceptions." He yanks one of the rocks free.

I shriek, fearing a slide that will bury us both. "What the hell are you doing?" I shout, racing to his side and slapping his hand from the rocks.

Dace turns to me, his face perfectly calm. "I think there's a cavern under here. I'd like to see if I'm right." He peers into the dark hole created by the missing rock. "Definitely something. Listen."

He yells into the opening. The sound reverberates for several seconds.

"You're loco." I back away. "Now look, I said I'd show you around. But I also promised to protect you. Back off and let's go around to the other side of this rock pile. There're likely to be some other creatures you can examine with your computer thingy."

"Alright," says Dace, reluctance sharpening his tone. He steps away from the rocks and strolls to his bike. "Let me grab some stuff first."

I yawn as I wait for him to collect his equipment. Although I was in bed early enough last night, I didn't sleep well. Spent too many hours planning every aspect of my escape from Eco.

We walk around to the opposite side of the rock pile. Dace keeps his eyes on the ground, undoubtedly searching for more creatures, while I stare absently at the horizon. As he kneels and takes samples of the thin soil, I sit down in the shade of the rocks and lean back against a large boulder that's in no danger of moving. Enjoying the coolness of the stone behind my back and the warm wind playing across my face, I close my eyes.

I wake to silence. Jumping to my feet, I stare wildly about. There's no sign of Dace.

The sun has dropped lower in the sky, telling me the afternoon is drifting toward dusk. I run around the perimeter of the rock pile, calling Dace's name, but receive no reply. The bikes and our supplies are just where we left them, except Dace's emergency kit is missing. I swear and dash to the section of the rock pile where Dace removed the stone.

Many more rocks have been pulled aside, forming a narrow opening no bigger than the width of a pair of slender shoulders. I run back to the bikes and fish a solar flashlight from my bag. Strapping my own emergency kit around my waist, I walk slowly toward the dark opening in the rocks.

I have no desire to step into that crevice, no inclination to follow Dace on his foolish expedition. But he's my responsibility as well as my only hope of getting my family off this godforsaken planet. I can't leave him no matter how much I'd like to.

Stupid boy.

Another stupid boy. More trouble than they're worth.

Dace's bright smile flashes through my mind. I take a deep breath and squeeze through the narrow opening, stepping into the darkness.

CHAPTER SIX

I flick on the flashlight. It casts a faint bluish glow as I pull out my holofone and check its illuminated screen. Of course, there's no signal. I suppose I should've called for help outside, but I really don't want to alert anyone to the situation unless absolutely necessary. Connor Patel might not be so eager to uphold his end of the bargain if he knows I lost his nephew on our very first day together.

I'm standing in a passage that's bigger than I'd anticipated. Although my head brushes the ceiling, I can stretch my arms wide and not touch the side walls. The rock that lines the passage is dark as rich soil, but flecked with something bright as silver. I focus my flashlight on the stone and the imbedded flakes glitter like finely polished metal.

The sharp scent of mineral-infused water fills my nostrils.

I creep forward, gripping my flashlight like the stun gun my grandfather taught me to use for protection. I wish I had that gun now, though I doubt there's anything in this cave I could use it on. Well, maybe one thing. I smile grimly as I consider using a stun gun on Dace.

The slope of the passage informs me I'm descending deeper below the surface. There's a faint sound I strain to identify—a gentle slap, like water washing against the side of a bowl. I follow the passage as it veers to the right and a gust of air blows against my head. Looking up, I spy a shaft that rises up through the rock ceiling. It must ascend to the surface, funneling air into the cave. At least I won't suffocate, although that might be preferable to being lost in a cavern with no food and little water.

Water. That's what I hear. Waves lapping against a shore. I shake my head. I've only heard such sounds on holodiscs. I must be imagining things.

I turn another corner and almost drop my flashlight. I've stepped into a large cavern, its domed rock roof pierced with air shafts that channel rays of light. The light pinpoints rough ledges and paths, and water—a still, clear body of water like a small underground lake. I'm standing at the top of a steeply inclined path leading down to the water and a rocky shore.

Dace is kneeling upon that shore, holding another monitoring device over the water.

"Mierda!" I make my way down to him, keeping a hand on the stone wall that edges one side of the path. "Just wander off and expect me to follow? You could've been killed instantly in a rock slide, you moron."

Dace looks up at me. There isn't even a flicker of contrition in his eyes. "But I wasn't." He holds up the monitoring device as I approach. "There are living creatures in this water, Ann. Did your colony know anything about that?"

"No." I stride over to him. "We knew there was water, of course. But creatures? How could that be?"

"Air, water, some form of food chain. Why not?" Dace pushes back the dark hair falling into his eyes. "I'm picking up traces of vegetation too. Water-based, but plants for sure. Not here, but drifting in from somewhere else." His eyes narrow as he examines the other side of the chamber, where the lake touches a stone wall. "I wonder … "

"Don't even think about getting in that water." I grab Dace's shoulder. "You've already pulled several idiotic stunts today. No more."

Dace yanks free of my grip. "You have no scientific curiosity."

"I have an instinct for self-preservation." I kneel beside him. "You seem to be lacking that gene." I stare into the lake. It appears dark, but only because I can see straight to the smooth black stones that line the bottom. "Your device must be malfunctioning. Nothing could live down here. It looks dead, and cold."

"It isn't." Dace leans forward and dabbles his fingers in the water. "Tepid, which is also strange." His gaze focuses on the opposite wall. "I'm betting there's more to see, behind that barrier. This is just a small overflow or outlet or something."

I extend one finger and touch the surface of the lake. It's much warmer than it looks. Not hot, but comfortable, like a cool bath. Sitting back on my heels, I stare at the tip of my finger, half-expecting some type of skin reaction. But the single drop of liquid glistens innocently.

"It's perfectly harmless," says Dace. He picks up a small fragment of rock from the shore and stuffs it in his pocket before rising to his feet. "I don't get it. No one's ever explored these caverns before? In all the time you've lived here, I'd have thought someone would've been curious."

I stand, shaking the dampness from the bottom of my jeans. "Curiosity gets people killed. My grandparents, for example. My mother's parents," I add, noting Dace's puzzled expression. "They were geologists, so of course they were interested in exploring the rock hills. But after they were killed in a slide no one else wanted to attempt it. I mean, we knew there was more water, but we had enough for our uses from the compound's wells. And after the terraforming went bust … " I shrug. "What was the point?"

"Exploration. Discovery." Dace fiddles with his gadget. "So I guess that wasn't high on the list of the colony's concerns."

"No, survival was more important. And my grandparents …" I shine the flashlight at the lake. "Well, they didn't die instantly, you see. They were trapped. For days and days. Trapped, injured, and suffocating. They recorded it all—for science, I guess." I shake my head. "My mother saw that holo file. The others tried to keep it from her, but she insisted, or so I'm told. It was all before I was born. My dad says it broke her."

Dace stuffs the digital monitor into the pouch strapped to his waist. "She doesn't seem broken to me."

"Yeah, I don't see it either." I keep my gaze focused on the lake. "But Dad always tells me that story when I complain about her. She's kind of a bitch, you know."

"That I can believe." Dace lays his fingers on my arm. "But very beautiful. I see where you get it from."

"Me?" I glance down at my hands, at the skin that's many shades darker than my mother's porcelain complexion. "I don't look like her. I take after my dad's side of the family."

He's staring at me with the strangest expression. I've seen Raid look at me with desire, and this isn't the same. But there's obvious admiration in those dark eyes.

"Your coloring, yes. But you have some of her features. I noticed that at dinner. Not the nose, though. You actually have a much more interesting nose. A regal profile." Dace swiftly turns his head aside. "Scientist, remember? Trained to observe. And also, I ... " He gazes out over the lake. "I like to do graphic stuff. On the computer."

"Art?" I raise my eyebrows. "You're an artist?"

Dace draws an invisible circle with one booted foot. "Don't know if I'd say that. But yeah, I like to create stuff. So I notice things—the way they look, the way the planes and angles ... " He stops speaking, tightening his lips.

"That's pretty cool." I think of the immersive games I've played with Raid and the others and consider that someone, somewhere, must have designed them. It's a curious thought, one I've never contemplated before. All those images—at one point, they were just an idea. Until someone's mind and hands brought them to life.

"We should go back," I say, after several minutes of staring at the placid lake in silence. "It's getting late."

"But we can return tomorrow?"

"I don't know." I turn to study Dace. He smiles, obviously trying to charm. It almost works. "Oh, I suppose. But you can't tell your uncle anything about this. Not yet. If my parents find out, they'll forbid me to escort you anywhere."

"Sworn to secrecy." Dace grabs my hand. "Thank you, Ann. You don't know how much this means to me."

"Oh, I think I do." I tighten my fingers around his. Partially in agreement, partially because I suspect Dace isn't accustomed to a girl's touch.

Proving my theory, a faint touch of color flushes his light brown skin.

"I really want to go to a real university," he says, not pulling his hand away. "More than anything."

"And I really want to get off of Eco," I reply, giving his hand a final squeeze before I release his fingers. "More than anything. Looks like we're on the same wavelength."

"Seems like it." Dace places the hand I'd gripped into his other hand and absently strokes his cradled fingers. "Hopefully we can both get what we want."

"That's the plan."

I turn as I hear a splash from the lake. "What's that?"

"Don't know." Dace steps close to the edge of the rocky shoreline.

As I reach to pull him back, there's another splash.

"Something's in there," says Dace under his breath.

From the center of the lake a form rises.

My fingers lock onto Dace's arm. I give a little yank. "Back."

The form takes shape, lifting its body half out of the water. It has a sleek head with the pointed snout of a dolphin, but the slick brown fur and front paws of an otter.

"Holy shit." Dace stumbles backward, almost knocking me over. I throw my arms around him to keep him on his feet.

The creature watches us with large, liquid brown eyes. There are no visible ears, but it cocks its head as if listening to some distant sound. With a wave of its solitary flipper tail, it leaps above the surface and dives back under.

"What the hell is that thing?" I shake Dace slightly. "Come on, naturalist. Explain."

"Don't have any idea." Dace leans back against my chest, breathing heavily.

"Wow, some insight there." I blow into his dark hair to force his head away from my face.

He lurches out of my arms, falling to his knees. Fumbling with his pouch, he pulls out a holofone. "Pictures," he mutters. "Must get pictures."

"It's probably gone."

"No, I don't think … "

Smooth and silent, the creature rises again from the water. Its eyes focus on Dace for a moment. It rears back as he holds out the fone and snaps several shots in succession. Spinning about, the creature dives and slaps its tail against the surface of the lake, sending a spray of water over our heads.

Dace instantly curls over his instrument pouch, shielding it with his body.

"Mierda!" I sputter, wiping my face with one hand.

Dace straightens and looks up at me. "You got the worst of it." A smile twitches the corners of his mouth.

"Shut it, Keeling. This is all your fault."

"I hope so," says Dace, rising to his feet. "I want to claim this discovery. Although," he adds, with a quick glance at my face, "I'm willing to share the glory."

"Glory?" I walk up to him, close enough to bump noses. "What's so glorious about some fish-things living under our feet?"

Dace stares into my eyes, his lower lip rolled into a pout, his chest heaving. "Damn, you're shallow, Ann Solano. Don't you have any sense of wonder? It's an entirely new species. Isn't that amazing enough for you? Think you're going to discover anything on Earth so unique? No, you won't. Earth's been explored and documented from one end to the other. This is new, really new."

I shove him back with one hand. "Don't lecture me. Sense of wonder? Yeah, I've got some. I wonder how I ended up on this godforsaken dead-end planet instead of Earth, where I belong. I wonder why I have no future. Take over the greenhouse from my grandmother—check. Marry some guy I've known all my life—check. Exciting future—hell no."

Dace eyes me, his expression shifting from anger to confusion. "But you have options … "

"No, I don't." I yank on strands of my damp, unraveling braid. "I don't have options. Not like you. Not unless I get off Eco."

"But this creature—who knows? Maybe it can mean something. Maybe it can help you, all of you."

"How?"

"Researchers will come here. To study it. That means new people, maybe lots of credits if they need to buy stuff … "

"Yeah, well, I prefer to take your uncle's offer and leave, thank you very much."

A splash. We turn to stare at the lake.

The creature has moved close to the rocky shore. I can clearly see its fish-like lower body and large, flexible tail fin. Dace moves forward as if drawn by an invisible string. He stretches out his fingers and touches the creature on its pointed snout. It opens its mouth.

I shriek and flail my arms, hoping to scare it away, but it simply examines us with bright eyes. Its open mouth displays rows of small but very pointed white teeth. I cross my arms in front of my chest and take two steps back.

A sound rings out—a reverberating sound, like a cacophony of bells.

I fall to the ground, heedless of the stone floor. Curling into a ball, I rock back and forth. That sound. That ringing sound— it travels throughout my body, like the steady pumping of my blood.

Light. Sun.

"Ann!" Dace's voice is faint, as if he stands at some distance, though I sense him kneeling beside me. He places his arm around my shoulders. "What is it? Are you okay?" A little shake. "Ann, talk to me!"

Below. Water.

"Make it stop!" I'm shouting and I don't know why. I pull away from Dace's arm and cover my ears with both hands.

Air. Above.

Another fountain of water washes over us. Sputtering, I open my eyes.

There's nothing in the lake but spreading ripples.

Dace crawls to the edge of the shore. He shakes his head and sends water flying in all directions. "Gone," he says, his voice suffused with wonder. "I think it's really gone. But where?" He raises his eyes and stares at the opposite side of the lake. "There must be a passage under that wall. A tunnel or something."

I'm still rocking slowly, gripping my knees to control the trembling in my limbs. "Shut up and help me get out of here. Now."

Dace jumps to his feet and moves swiftly to my side. He thrusts out his hand. "Grab hold."

I take his fingers in a tight grip and he pulls me to my feet.

Dace looks me up and down before whipping off this jacket. "Here, this should fit. It's yours, after all."

"I have a jacket," I say, once I still my chattering teeth.

"Now you have two." Dace drapes the jacket around my shoulders. "What happened to you, anyway?" He motions for me to walk ahead of him as we move toward the inclined pathway.

"Don't know." I pull the jacket close about me, glad it's made of a fabric that repels water. My jeans cling to my legs, chafing my thighs with every step. "But when that thing made noise, it was as if it went all through me." I glance over my shoulder. "You didn't feel anything?"

"No. I heard the sounds, of course. But it just seemed like barks and whistles to me, with some keening thrown into the mix. I did record a bit." He pats at his waist. "Flicked on the holo. Hope it picked up the noises through the pouch."

"Damn, Dace." I turn my head and focus on placing one foot before the other. "You could think of that, but ignore the fact I was, like, writhing on the ground?"

"I ran to you as fast as I could."

"After you got your recording." I sigh in relief as we reach the entrance to the cave.

"Well, I didn't know if I'd ever have another chance … "

"Never mind. I get it—scientist first, always. No wonder you act like you've never kissed a girl." I slide through the narrow opening and step into the light.

And promptly slump to the ground, falling into a different type of darkness.

CHAPTER SEVEN

Fingers move over my face, coming to rest on my lips. "Ann? Ann, are you breathing?"

"Could I answer if I wasn't?" I swat Dace's hand away.

"You passed out."

"Yeah, genius, I did." I struggle to a sitting position. "How long was I out?"

Dace stretches his arm behind my back to brace me. "Only a minute or two. Here—some water." He hands me his flask.

After a few sips I pass it back to him, meeting his concerned gaze. "I'm okay. Must've gotten too hot or something."

"Hot?" Dace snorts. "Hardly. It wasn't warm in there, and anyway, we're still pretty wet." He fixes his brown eyes intently on my face. "Something happened in there, when the creature voiced those sounds. What was it?"

I snap the band holding my plait together and begin unweaving my damp hair. "Thought I heard something. Weird, like bells. Not what you heard, I guess."

"No." Dace adjusts his arm so I can lean against his shoulder. "Told you—I just heard whistles and barks. No bells, that's for sure."

"Well, not bells exactly, but reverberating, you know?" I sigh and run my fingers through my loose hair. "Guess you don't. It was this strange sound that seemed to seep into my bones. And … " I glance over at Dace from under my lashes, "There was something else."

There's the color rising in his face again. "What else?" He glances up and over my head.

"Words. No, not words exactly. But the meaning, the sense of ideas. Thoughts."

"Your thoughts, or something else?" Dace asks, his eyes widening.

"Not mine. And not fully formed. Just this flicker, like an outline or concept." I feel a tremor ripple through his shoulder. "Something about the sun, and light, and … " I search my memory. "Above. Some idea of above."

Dace says nothing. He simply searches my face for a moment, as if trying to see into me, to study me on a subatomic level.

"So what's that mean, scientist guy?" I laugh, trying for lighthearted and hearing instead a trill of nervous agitation.

"Not sure." Dace drops his arm and leans forward, reaching for his discarded equipment pouch. "Can I try something?" He holds up the device he used on the insect and lizard creatures.

I adjust my position on the hard ground. "Gonna put me in a bubble?"

"If you don't mind." Dace stands and holds out the device, waving it about like a wizard's wand.

"Not sure, but go ahead." I pull my knees to my chest.

A shimmer of gold swirls about me, casting a veil of light around my body. When I look toward Dace, I can see only a shadow moving beyond the globe that envelops me.

As swiftly as it appeared, the light dissipates and everything comes back into focus. Dace's slender form is clearly etched against the pale gray of the evening sky. I watch as he manipulates the device with several taps and swipes of his finger.

"Anything interesting?" I rise to my feet, slapping at the dust shining like diamonds against the dark blue of my damp jeans.

Dace continues to stare into the small monitor, his fingers obviously manipulating data and images. After a few minutes, he looks up at me.

His eyes hold awe and wonder—the same expression that lit his face when we first saw the water creature. "Ann," he says, in a voice that cracks with excitement, "it's the same. Just a little bit, just a tiny snip of genetic coding, but … "

"What the hell are you yapping about?" I stride forward, ripping the device from his hands. There are two images placed side-by-side on the screen. I know little of genetic markers, but even I can see a similarity—one significant spike in each image. "So what are these?"

"One of them is info I got from the water creature. The other one is … you."

I stare at him. "That's ridiculous," I say at last. "Impossible. I'm human. That thing isn't. Hell, it isn't like anything on Earth. You said so yourself."

"I know."

"Your data must be corrupted."

"It isn't." Dace slides the device back into the equipment pouch. "Your DNA displays a snippet of genetic code that matches that creature. Probably the reason you felt a connection when it voiced those sounds. You heard something else, some type of direct communication."

I walk toward him, placing one foot in front of the other in measured, precise steps. Standing directly before him, I lean forward and grab the fabric of his shirt with both hands.

"You will tell no one." I pull him close, until his face is only inches from mine. "Understand?"

"I must." Dace's whole body goes rigid. "It's an amazing discovery. No way I'll hide it."

I loosen one hand's hold on his shirt and smooth the crumpled fabric. "Just for now. Just for a little while." I allow my fingers to slide up his chest, to rest under his chin. "You can put it all in your report, once you leave Eco. Use it to get a scholarship, I don't care. But don't tell anyone yet." I stroke his jawline with one finger. "Okay?"

Dace swallows hard. "Why do you care? You're probably not alone, you know. I bet whatever caused the mutation is tied to being born and raised on this planet. So everyone except the first colonists would be affected."

"I don't care about everyone." I let go of his shirt and step back.

Released from my grip, Dace sways on his feet for a second. "I mean, you're no different than most people on Eco. You're not a freak or anything." He rubs absently at his jaw, his eyes never leaving my face.

"I would be, on Earth." I return his steady gaze. "Wouldn't I? Maybe they wouldn't even allow me, or my parents, to land. Not if they knew. Can you promise me that wouldn't happen? I've seen the holodiscs, I know all about the genetic purity laws."

"If they tested you ... "

"But why would they? Unless someone alerts the authorities, we're in the clear. My family has the proper documentation, passed down by my grandparents. Certified one-hundred-percent human. And since my parents were born of those humans, they can claim all human rights, as can I."

Dace sucks in a deep breath. "I want to study the creatures some more."

"And you can. I'll escort you back here every day. Hell, you can gather six billion terabytes of data for all I care. Just don't squeal to anyone about me. Not until my family and I are living on Earth."

Dace examines me—dispassionately, as if calculating my mass. "But once they know, they'll deport you."

Damn his logic. "I'll worry about that when the time comes." I hold out my hand. "Promise me you'll stay quiet about this, just for now, and I swear you'll have access to the caverns every day you're on Eco."

"But Ann, don't you want to know what this means? I could run tests ... "

Do I want to know? This tiny change that turns my entire world upside down—do I want to know what it means, how it might affect me in the future?

"No." I thrust out my hand again. "Promise."

Dace wraps his fingers around mine. "Okay. I promise. For now. Until I can write up the full report."

"Until my family and I are living on Earth." I squeeze his fingers.

Dace gives a curt nod. "Until then."

I drop his hand and step back with a smile. "Let's grab the bikes and get a move on. It's late. Your uncle will think I've already lost you."

"Ann," says Dace, as we stroll toward the bikes, "it isn't a curse, you know. It's more like a miracle."

I grab my helmet by its strap. Allowing it to swing from my fingers I face Dace over the backs of the bikes. "Let me set you straight, Dacian Keeling. No one on Eco would agree with you. No one. In fact … " a new strategy flashes into my mind, "there are quite a few colonists who'd kill you to keep something like that quiet. We're proud to be human, you know. It's one of our only sources of pride. Not something most colonists want smashed to hell."

Dace pops on his helmet, flipping up the visor so he can speak. "Is that a threat?"

"Not from me. Others … " I shrug before donning my own helmet.

Slamming down his visor, Dace throws the bike into gear. He speeds off before I can even mount my bike.

I doubt he'll get lost, as the windmills' blades are clearly visible on the horizon. But I don't want him to arrive back at the compound too long before me. Despite his promise, I plan to keep a close eye on Dacian Keeling.

CHAPTER EIGHT

In the small mirror that hangs above our bathroom sink, I examine my face. I look perfectly human of course. There's nothing in my appearance that betrays the fact I may harbor a snippet of alien DNA.

"May" being the operative word. I'm still not convinced Dace's theory is sound. I stick out my tongue. My mirror image mimics me, down to the blemish that reddens the side of my distinctive nose. Yeah, beautiful, that's me.

I wrinkle my nose at my reflection and turn away. It's time to track down Dace and make him run that data again. I just don't believe simply being conceived and born on this planet is enough to alter anyone's genetic code. It's not like we eat produce grown in its dirt.

The water. We drink the water.

I mutter obscenities as I yank a brush through my loose hair. I fling a light jacket over my T-shirt and spare the mirror one more glance.

Alien. Not entirely human. No—that isn't me. That can't be me.

My dad's camped out in our living area, hunched over the dining table, examining some digital plans.

I take hold of his arm as I peer over his shoulder. "Terraforming machines, huh? Looking for some parts for Captain Patel? I thought most of that stuff was already torn apart and dispersed."

"Most." Dad reaches up to pat at my hand. "We kept that one digger together. You know; you've seen it. At the back of the storage shed."

"Oh, the old rusted thing?"

Dad swipes one finger across the monitor and the plans bloom in three dimensions. Hovering above the monitor, a digital replica of the huge excavator spins at my father's touch. "Your mother thinks we should sacrifice the fans from the digger, but I disagree. It's still operational. I don't think we should tear it down. Who knows when our wells might run dry? We may need to excavate for additional water."

Water again. I almost mention the underground lake, but bite my tongue in time. "What about all those other junk parts lying about the shed? Surely there's something in that jumble Captain Patel can use."

"That's my thought as well." Dad glances up at me with a smile. "Going to hang out with your friends? I imagine they're over at the rec hall, since it's well past the dinner hour."

"Maybe." I can't help but smile in return. "You should take a break too. You've been staring at this stuff all day."

Dad touches one part of the holographic plans, zooming in on a particular section. "Not much else to do at the moment. Everyone's deserted me. Your grandparents are out taking a walk. You know how they love their evening walks."

"Yeah." I push back the hair that's tumbling over my shoulders. "Where's Mom?"

"Don't have any idea." Dad's tone is nonchalant, but I'm not fooled. "She disappeared as soon as the dinner table was cleared. Which, by the way," he gently bumps my arm with his fist, "you didn't offer to help with."

"I know. Sorry." I lean in and kiss him on the cheek. "I'll do better tomorrow, I promise."

"Your promises, chica … " My dad shakes his head. "Anyway, don't stay out too late. You're supposed to escort Patel's nephew again tomorrow, right?"

"Yep." I step back, fiddling with a strand of my hair. "He's all right. Very serious and kind of … young for his age. One thing's for sure, Papa—you don't have to worry about him. Trying to take advantage, I mean."

"I'm not—he seems like a rather reserved young man. Not like your granddad's apprentice." Dad shakes his head. "Him, sometimes, I worry about."

"Raid? Oh, he isn't so bad." I move toward the hall, but pause in the open doorway. "Anyway, I thought everyone had already married us off."

"Not me." Dad pulls his hand through the holographic

excavator, crumpling it into a ball of light that melts back into the monitor. He turns to look at me. "I'm not ready for you to marry anyone." He studies me for a moment, a shadow flitting across his face. "You've grown up so fast. I can't believe you'll be eighteen next year. Anyway," he turns his attention back to the now two-dimensional plans, "there's plenty of time for you to decide who you want to marry, or if you want to marry at all. Don't rush it, chica."

Like I did. I know that's what he's thinking, though he'll never speak those words. My parents married when they were only eighteen, and while I'm almost sure my father still loves my mother, I suspect there are many days when he questions why.

"I'm in no hurry." I blow him a kiss before I leave the room. "See you later, Papa."

"Have fun," he replies, his attention already captured by his work.

***

I make my way outside, jogging across the quiet yard to the gate that opens to the landing strip. The Augusta Ada sits on the tarmac, dark and hulking as a hibernating beast. Before I head to the recreation hall I want to check in with Dace, to see what he's up to. Just to make sure that he isn't blabbing our secret to everyone in the colony.

I trudge up the steep ramp that leads into the belly of the

Ada. One of the crew, obviously on guard duty, eyes me as I step into the cargo hold. His unnaturally blue eyes betray his status as a cyber, a human whose body's been substantially enhanced with implants or prosthetics. I'm always startled by his kind. Their otherness sets something fluttering in my stomach. Logically I know this is foolish—they're still human, mostly. I also know cybers don't choose to replace original body parts with digital implants and prostheses. Most are former soldiers, severely injured during their stint in the military. The restoration of their bodies is a reward for their service.

But they never receive the restoration of their full human status.

I stare at the man as this realization slams into my mind. Emie makes this point often enough, but it never really sank in until now. "I'm here to see Dace. Is he anywhere about?"

"Dunno." The man gestures toward a tall woman standing in the shadows. "Calla might have some idea."

The woman steps forward. Her pale hair, streaked with green highlights, is cropped short, and her features display the inhuman perfection of a doll.

I gnaw on my lower lip, wondering where and how this woman's original face was destroyed. A fire, perhaps, or an explosion. Not an uncommon danger for a soldier or any other spacer.

"Haven't seen the boy," says Calla. Her voice is artificially enhanced as well.

I shiver, envisioning the horror of an accident that could inflict such damage. It must've been hell—the pain of the treatment on top of the original injury, the terrible sense of loss. "Do you mind if I check his quarters? I'm his guide around Eco, and I'd like to chat with him before tomorrow." I slowly extend my arm. "Ann Solano."

Calla makes no move to take my hand. "I know who you are. Had to vet you, didn't we?" She looks me over. "Guess it's all right. Move along, then." With a flick of her gloved hand she motions toward the back of the cargo bay. "Through there. Down the hall and make a right. First hatch."

I walk past the two cybers without looking directly at them.

Stepping into the narrow hall is like entering a drainage pipe. Dull metal plates cover the sides and curve to form an arched ceiling. I shake off the sensation that the walls are pressing in on me. If I'm lucky enough to get passage on this ship I'll have to get used to the close quarters.

The first hatch stands open, blocking the view into Dace's berth. I peer through the sliver of space between door and frame, then step back.

Mom is standing in Dace's room, next to a built-in shelf. She's balancing something in her palm, turning her hand this way and that to examine the object. It looks like the mineral sample Dace brought back from the cave. That's strange enough—my mother on this ship, in a young man's quarters, fondling his belongings. Even odder is she's not alone.

Captain Connor Patel is standing beside her. Standing very close.

I position myself where I can watch without being seen.

"So, you think it might be worth further study?" Patel lays

his palm over the rock sample, covering my mother's delicate fingers with his large hand.

"Oh, definitely." Mom glances up at him, flashing a smile as bright as Eco's sun. "I've never seen anything like it. I'd like to examine it in more detail, with some of my parents' equipment. Do you think your nephew would mind if I borrowed this piece? Just for tonight, you understand."

"I'm sure he'd be fine with that." Connor Patel stares into my mother's hazel eyes as if he's just sighted the lost moon of Arias.

I clamp my lips together to trap the swear words in my mouth.

"Well," Mom tilts her head and gazes into Patel's face, "I don't want to cause any trouble."

"Don't you?" The captain's voice takes on a teasing tone. "I'd have thought trouble was something you enjoyed."

Mom's golden eyebrows arch over her wide eyes. "Now, whatever gave you that impression, Captain Patel?"

"Connor."

"Only if you call me Tara. Ms. Cooper sounds so formal." Mom slides her fingers from his grip and pockets the rock sample. "So, you think I like trouble, Connor?"

"I think you may *be* trouble," replies the captain.

He's got that right. I clench my fingers into fists.

"And trouble concerns you?" My mom gives a little pout before those lovely lips curl into another smile.

Connor Patel runs a hand through his thick, dark hair. "Let's just say it confuses me."

"There shouldn't be any confusion." My mother leans into

him and runs her fingers down his arm. "I thought I was being rather transparent, actually."

As I prepare to scream, I hear whistling behind me. Spinning about, I spy Dace stepping into the hall.

I hurry to meet him, careful not to stomp on the metal floors. The last thing I want is for Dace to find my mother and his uncle in his cabin. Dace isn't stupid. He might put two and two together. "Hey," I say, reaching him before he can move farther down the corridor, "Just looking for you. Come to the rec hall—I want you to meet some of the other kids."

"I was headed to my room … "

"Hell no, that's way too boring." I usher him toward the large hatch. "You don't want to just sit in your room. You'll go bonkers. Besides, it's early yet."

"I wasn't going to bed," replies Dace, shooting me an inquisitive glance. "I thought I'd run some more tests on my samples."

"Plenty of time for that." I shove him into the cargo bay. "I want to introduce you to some of my friends. They'll be thrilled. We don't get many young spacers."

"Those two guys we ran into earlier didn't seem too thrilled." Dace jerks his arm to shake off my hand. "And I am not a spacer."

"Oh, I know. Just that you've been traveling from planet to planet. They'll want to hear about that. I mean, we're just stuck here on Eco. Not much to talk about."

As we stride past Calla, the cyber glances up from polishing her laser pistol. "Found each other, did you? Now what?"

"Off to meet some other people, or so I'm told," says Dace,

with a jerk of his head towards me.

A grin, macabre in its artificiality, splits Calla's face. "Taking charge, is she? Well, enjoy it, little man. Not often you get to spend time with the young, pretty ones."

Dace straightens, the flush in his cheeks contrasting with his dignified expression. "Ann's simply introducing me to some of her friends. No big deal, but it's something different, you know?"

Calla laughs, a mechanical trill that turns into a wheeze. "Yeah, I gotcha. Well, run along. I'll clue in the Captain if he questions your whereabouts."

"We'll be in the recreation hall." Determined, I meet Calla's direct gaze without faltering.

"Sure thing." Calla waves us away with one sweep of her gloved hand. "Better get a move on. Captain's likely to show up any minute with a list of chores for the kid."

Knowing how my mother's entranced him, I doubt it. I just pray the cyber won't go searching the ship. That's all I need— someone else discovering my mother's little rendezvous with Captain Patel. Gossip swirls about the colony like a sandstorm. All it takes is one word, even from a cyber, and my dad and grandparents will hear all about it.

"Come on." I grab Dace's hand and pull him toward the exterior ramp. "No time like the present to become the most popular person on Eco."

"Or the most uncomfortable," Dace replies without enthusiasm. But he doesn't yank his hand away.

CHAPTER NINE

The rec hall is full of people. I lead Dace to the game room, threading our way through a cluster of chairs. I nod silent greetings to the adults who are gathered before a large screen, engrossed in watching an old film.

"Classic movie night," I tell Dace. "We stream them from the servers. One of the original colonists brought a digital collection of every film still in existence."

"2-D," observes Dace, turning to stare back at the faces filling the screen.

"Well, yeah. I said they were classics." I don't mention that the colonist who brought the files was my grandmother. My mom's mother, whom I never knew. But sometimes, watching her collection of movies, I feel as if I've glimpsed some part of her.

The door to the game room's closed, blocking the noise of the younger colonists' immersive holo games from the main part of the building. I knock, loudly.

The door swings back and I stare up into Raid's face. "Hello. Thought I'd bring Dace by to meet everyone. You mind?"

"Why should I?" Raid steps back to allow us to enter the room. Closing the door behind him, he turns and leans against its thick metal panels.

"No reason." I motion for Dace to take a seat on the low sofa. "So, how's things?" I meet Raid's speculative expression with a smile.

"Things are fine." Raid looks me up and down. "Dragged junior scientist all over Eco today?"

"I did."

"Had fun?"

"Not sure I'd call it that." From the corner of my eye I see one of the younger girls plop down and press up next to Dace. She chatters and shoots him demure looks from beneath her fluttering lashes. He appears distinctly uncomfortable. "Maybe I'd better go to the rescue."

Raid takes hold of my wrist. "I'm sure nature boy can handle Marissa. Now," his fingers glide up my arm, coming to rest on my shoulder. "Let's talk. Things have been kind of nuclear lately—between you and me, I mean. You know I don't wanna fight with you." He caresses my shoulder as he turns me to face him.

"You can start by dropping the rude crap around Dace." I meet his intense stare with a steady gaze of my own. "He's okay. A little obsessed ... "

"Says the girl who only thinks about leaving Eco." Raid leans in to press his forehead against mine.

I could leap in and happily drown in those dark eyes. "And you don't ever consider it?"

"Mmmm … sometimes. But what's the point in living our whole lives for the future?" Raid dips his head until his lips are almost brushing mine. "Live for now. Tomorrow may never come."

I should move, but I don't. I allow Raid to kiss me—a slow, sensual kiss that forces me to grab his arms to keep from wobbling.

"Everyone's watching," I say, when he pulls away for a second.

"Good. Maybe they'll learn something," Raid replies, and kisses me again.

"Bien, enough." I step back when Raid comes up for air. "I better check on Dace. I brought him here knowing he'd be assaulted by the younger girls. And Emie, if Kam ever steps away. Now, don't give me that look. He's my responsibility."

Raid frowns. "Your supposed ticket out of here, you mean."

"Yes, that too." I study his glowering face. "Maybe, if the captain changes his mind and agrees to take us, you could come along. I'm sure we could squeeze in one more passenger."

"And leave all this?" As Raid throws out his hand to indicate the crowded game room, a holographic laser slices through his chest.

"Score!" Yells Kam. "You're dead meat, widget-maker."

"Not playing, asswipe. Clean your goggles," replies Raid, with a glance over his shoulder. He looks back at me while Kam colorfully protests. "What the hell—go see what your new pal's up to, Ann. But find me later." He leans in and gives me a quick kiss before turning to Kam. "Now I'm in the game. Prepare for annihilation, Frye."

I gaze after Raid's tall form for a moment then shake my head and make my way to the couch. I really shouldn't allow Raid to kiss me like that, not when I plan on leaving. But I do love those kisses—they send a current zipping from my heart out to all my fingers and toes.

"Ann!" Dace's voice cuts through my reverie. He looks up at me with desperation.

"Move over," I tell Marissa, right before flopping onto the couch. The younger girl squeaks in protest as I wiggle between her and Dace.

"We were talking." Her lower lip pokes out.

"No, *you* were talking." I use my elbow to shove her toward the sofa arm. "So, how're you doing?" I ask Dace.

"Going deaf," he replies. "At least in one ear."

"Yeah, Marissa likes to talk. And talk, and talk." I ignore the daggers Marissa's eyes cast my way. "But she's kinda hot, huh?"

Dace blushes as Marissa squawks something about "shriveled bitches" and jumps to her feet. She prances over to Raid and Kam, who studiously ignore her.

"Anyway, since Marissa was pretty much monopolizing you, I thought I'd better head over and do the official introduction thing." I stick two fingers in my mouth and whistle. "Hey, space-rats, listen up! We've got a guest."

All eyes in the room focus on Dace. "Hello," he says, with a forced smile.

"This is Dace. Well, Dacian Keeling, but he goes by Dace.

He's the nephew of Captain Patel of the Augusta Ada."

"Yeah." Trent slaps his gamer headpiece against his palm. "We heard that. Everyone already knows, Solano."

Of course they do. This is Eco, the small town of planets. I shoot Trent a silencing look. "Anyway, Dace is a scientist. A naturalist, to be exact. He's studying the plants and animals of all the places the Ada visits."

Kam saunters forward, still wearing his gamer gloves. I glance over his shoulder, expecting to see Emie, but it appears she's left the room. That's odd. She must've slipped out the back door.

"Will find crap-all here," says Kam.

Dace shakes his head. "Saw some pretty unique things today. Lizard-like creatures and some flying insects. That was interesting."

Kam sneers. "Those things? Damned annoying is all they are. Especially the bugs. Bet I've killed hundreds of them, working on the windmills. Give a slap and swat them up against the blades. Splat!" He spread his hands out as he stands over us, gazing down.

I expect the younger boy to shrink away, but Dace sits up straighter. "How very brave."

Kam's face turns almost as red as his hair. "Now look, spacer … "

I rise to my feet. "Anyway, if anyone has questions for Dace—you know, about other planets or Earth or whatever—now's the time to ask."

"Chill," says Raid, stepping up behind Kam. He grabs the redhead's elbow and pulls him to the side. "Let nature boy talk. Might learn something." He perches on the sofa arm. "Stop swearing and take a load off, Kam. Still plan to wipe the floor with your sorry ass later."

"You're from Earth?" Trent breaks through the cluster of young people.

"Yes, originally," says Dace. He's keeping an eye on Kam, who's skulked off to the far side of the room.

Trent plops into a pile of cushions near Dace's feet. "Where'd you live?"

"India. Mumbai. My mom still lives there. I'll go back, eventually, when I can get into a decent university. That's what the research is for, you see. To prove I'm worth a scholarship."

"Mumbai, really? That's funny—you don't look entirely Indian," observes Marissa as she sidles up to Raid.

I give her a warning look as I sit back down, but Dace answers with equanimity. "I'm not. My dad was English, or American. Not really sure. Never met him, so who knows?"

"Your mom should." Marissa's displaying her usual lack of tact. Raid gently pushes her aside and she slumps into one of the gamer chairs.

Dace shrugs. "She doesn't like to talk about him, and I don't like to ask. Doesn't matter anyway. Bastard disappeared before I was born. On the other hand—my uncle, he's always been there for us. Even when he was in the military, and then crewing on other traders, he sent us money and visited. More than my so-called father's ever done."

I study Dace as he delivers this information, recognizing the bitterness lacing his tone. He's not as resigned to these facts as he likes to pretend. Glancing over his head, I catch Raid's eye. His serious expression isn't a surprise. Raid's father died many years ago after a minor accident led to a major infection that no medicine on Eco could cure. The fact that his mother is one of our medics only makes the situation worse, since she still blames herself for her husband's death.

"So, it's really as hard to get into a university as we hear?" asks Trent.

Dace nods. "Yes. Unless you're wealthy. Or your family went to a particular school. Which, of course, they couldn't have done unless they were wealthy. So, yeah—easy for the rich. The rest of us are pretty much screwed."

"Well, that leaves us out, too," observes Raid, giving me a significant look. "Even if we lived on Earth, we wouldn't have the credits to go."

"You never know." I twirl a strand of my hair about one finger. "It sure would be a lot easier there. At least there are universities. All we have are holodiscs"

"And the 'sphere," adds Trent.

"Which we can't even access half the time."

If Emie were here, she'd call me on that comment, since part of her job involves maintaining our connection to the galaxy-wide web of communication satellites, space stations, and ship-to-ship relays. Of course, even though she takes it personally, it isn't Emie's fault our system doesn't always work, leaving us without access to the 'sphere for months at a time. Just another consequence of being stuck on Eco.

"Don't kid yourself—that's all most people on Earth have." Dace turns to me, his dark eyes shadowed by thick lashes. "Like I said, not much chance for anyone who isn't part of the upper echelon."

"So, what's it like?" Lily flops down beside Trent. "Earth, I mean. We've seen the holodiscs, and movies, and other stuff, but that doesn't really show the way most people live, I bet."

Dace leans into the sofa cushions. "No, it doesn't." He tilts his head back and stares at the metal ceiling. "Most people live in crowded cities, sharing tiny apartments with lots of other people. Sometimes family or friends, sometimes whomever they can find to help pay for a place. They work at any job they can find, or—if they're lucky—take over the job they inherited from their parents. They watch holodiscs and play games, just like you. Pretty much live through their computers most of the time. There are some sports, but you have to be pretty good to get onto a team, even an amateur one." Dace drops his head and gazes at his now rapt audience. "No one moves around much. Too hard, with all the laws. You have to have documents for everything. Most people have them implanted." He points to a tiny scar on his right forearm. "Easier. You just get scanned when you go anywhere that requires docs."

"That doesn't sound very nice," says one of the youngest girls.

"Oh, don't get me wrong, I still love the Earth. It's my home. But it has its problems. Mainly," Dace glances over at me, "there's no real opportunity for anyone who isn't already wealthy or powerful. Whatever social strata you're born into, you're pretty much stuck there."

I meet his gaze with a frown. Everyone's always telling me my dreams of life on Earth aren't realistic. Bien, so what? I dig my fingers into the fabric of the sofa. I know Earth is not a paradise, but hell, neither is Eco. At least it will be different. At least on

Earth I may have a chance to break free of a future that feels like it's all done and decided. Maybe Dace thinks no one can rise above their beginnings on Earth, but Dace doesn't know me very well.

And he doesn't know my mother at all. If anyone can soar beyond a social barrier, she can.

Raid kicks at the sofa frame. "That's why so many join the military, or sign up with the companies looking for space rats, I guess."

"Yeah." Dace looks around the room. "Like your grandparents did, I suspect. Bet there's not much of the upper echelon out here."

"None," says Raid. "We're all mongrels."

I shoot him a glance. "Speak for yourself."

"Oh yeah, Ann." Sarcasm sharpens Raid's voice. "Your grandparents were rich, were they? Nah, didn't think so. My family might hail from the Himalayas but yours were mountain people too—the Andes and Appalachia, right? Not exactly Rio or Paris."

I refuse to look at him. He's right, but I can't believe it'll mean that much on Earth these days, despite Dace's obviously prejudiced opinions.

"But what about all the wilderness and parks and things?" asks Trent. "There's still lots of unspoiled land on Earth, right? I mean, that's what I've seen on the 'sphere."

"Still there." Dace frowns. "But most people can't visit those places. Restricted access. Have to be part of the right groups to travel there, and most of us aren't. There are holo cams and viewing facilities, of course. You can feel as if you're traveling to certain spots, for a price. Some people do that if they have a bit of extra credit. Of course, if you have enough, you can buy huge estates or entire islands. Or even a small country. But most people," he shrugs, "just live in the same neighborhood, in their little apartments or shacks, all their lives. Not many ways to get rich unless you've already got some credits to start with."

"Maybe we're better off on Eco." Trent's beautiful face grows pensive.

"Sure." I scoot forward until I'm perched on the edge of the sofa. "Because we have so many options here."

"Anyway, it is what it is." Dace taps me on the arm. "But, enough about Earth. I'm happy to have landed here on Eco, collecting lots of great data, thanks to Ann."

"So you work for a corporation already?" Marissa stares at him with renewed interest.

"No, but all this research will win me a spot at a major university. Once I have a degree, I can get a job with a great company and then … everything will open up for me." A sheepish smile crosses Dace's face. "That's the plan, anyway."

"Sounds like a load of crap to me." Kam steps out of the shadows. "Like some kiddie science project's gonna win you a spot at one of the rich brats' finishing schools. Yeah, that's freakin' likely. They don't want our kind there, spacer, no matter how smart we might be."

"There are scholarships." Dace doesn't wilt under Kam's bitter smile.

"For their friends. Or maybe if you screw the right people."

"Shut it, Kam." I muster my most threatening expression—the

one that mimics my grandmother's glare. "Young kids present."

Kam snorts. "Like they never hear such crap in this tin can colony. Okay, Solano, I'll shut up. I'd like to get back to crushing Raid, anyway. Enough of this shit." He turns and strides over to the game console. Flipping the switch that restarts the game, he shoulders his laser tag rifle. "Ready to get some action going, widget-maker?"

"It's on, power-jockey." Raid leaps to his feet and strides to the middle of the room, facing Kam. Marissa and most of the others follow and surround the two young men as they prepare for battle.

I shake my head. "Boys and toys." I glance at Dace. "Sorry. Didn't mean you. You seem more sensible than most."

Dace smiles. "I don't know. I like my virtual games too. But I wouldn't take on those two. They're pretty bad-ass."

"So, you think what you've found on Eco's really going to help with your research?" Trent slides his cushion a little closer to the sofa.

Dace's face lights up. "Oh yes, especially with what we saw in the cavern … "

I press my foot over his instep. Dace grunts and shoots me a surprised glance.

"What cavern?" Trent looks from Dace to me and back again. "There's a cavern?"

"No, I … " Dace's eyes widen.

I grab his flailing hands and pull him close to me. "Cavern? You mean that tiny cave under the rock pile? Where you spied those lizards?"

Out of the corner of my eye I observe Trent's stubborn expression.

"Lizards are everywhere," he says. "And Dace said cavern. You talking crap, Ann?"

"No, of course not." I yank Dace forward until we're nose to nose. "Dace is disoriented. Must've gotten too much sun today. Scrambled his brains."

Dace jerks my hands. "Wait a minute, there was a cavern … "

Before Dace can say another word, I lean forward and kiss him, full on the lips.

I make it a good kiss—a long, lingering kiss that will shut him up for the foreseeable future.

"Damn," says a familiar voice. "That was fast."

I pull away from Dace and stare up into a pair of flashing dark eyes. Raid's standing in front of the couch, still holding his laser rifle.

"Mierda," I mutter.

Dace drops back against the sofa cushions, his face a study in confusion.

"Game over," Raid yells to Kam. Tossing his rifle to Trent, who clutches it to his chest in astonishment, Raid strides toward the back of the game room. He sheds his headpiece and gloves as he goes, dashing them to the floor.

"What was that all about?" Dace is staring at me, his brown eyes very wide in his narrow face.

"Nothing." The back door slams. I toss my hair over my shoulder. "You were sitting there, looking all serious and scientific and stuff and I just had this urge to kiss you. Mind?"

"No, I mean, I'm not sure ... " Dace jumps to his feet. "I think I'll go back to the ship now." He speaks with exaggerated dignity, tugging down his rumpled shirt. "I'll meet you tomorrow, at the front gate. What time?"

"Eight, if that's okay."

"Fine." Dace strolls off, exiting through the main door.

I catch Trent staring at me. "What're you looking at?"

"You kissed him. I thought you and Raid ... "

"People around here are too freakin' interested in other people's business." I stand, looking about for Emie. There's still no sign of her, which is weird, especially since Kam hasn't left the room. "See you later, kid. Need to find my friend."

"Which one?" asks Trent.

I leave, but not before chucking a pillow at him.

CHAPTER TEN

I walk through pools of light cast by our solar lamps, stepping from shadow to light and back into darkness. Near the front doors of the greenhouse I spy a couple lounging on a discarded crate. My heart slams into my ribcage, but of course it's not my mother. She'd never do something so foolish. It's just Karla and Caroline. Entwined in each other's arms, they're oblivious to my presence. I hurry on, not wanting to disturb them.

I wander aimlessly. Emie's probably in her family quarters, grabbing some rest after a long day. Her apprenticeship to Ivana, our computer and communications expert, is quite demanding, especially since Ivana doesn't believe in things like breaks or lunch.

Reaching the back gate, I climb its metal rungs and stare over the top rail toward the Augusta Ada. A light shines, illuminating the cargo hold. I identify Calla, her blonde head easily recognizable amid the clutter of dark boxes. Next to her, perched on a crate, sits Emie.

"Your friend seems to have a fascination with cybers."

I turn my head to face my mother.

"She thinks they're victims of discrimination." I jump off the gate.

"Interesting." Mom is backlit by the solar lamps, the light turning her fair hair into a halo. "She's plotting a social revolution?"

"On Eco? Not likely." I grip one of the gate's smooth metal rails for support. "You're out late."

My mother's gentle smile is more brutal than a slap in the face. "Couldn't sleep. Thought I needed a bit of exercise. So," she tilts her head to examine me, "where's that boyfriend of yours? Or have you thrown him over for Connor's nephew?"

So she isn't trying to hide their first-name basis. "Oh, Raid was playing some game with Kam." I refrain from mentioning he stalked off before I left the room. "And I think Dace went back to the ship. We plan to head out early tomorrow."

Mom moves closer. "You know, Ann, I'm very grateful you took Connor's offer. Of course, I'm aware you've always been as desperate as I am to get off Eco, but still—escorting the nephew about, I appreciate that."

"Dace," I say, eyeing my mother with suspicion. "His name's Dace, not 'the nephew.'"

"Right." She reaches me and leans against the fence, one slender hand curled about a gate rail, the other resting on my shoulder. "Dace. Funny name." Her hazel eyes sweep over my face. "Anyway, I'm glad you managed to grab the opportunity. If I'm not mistaken, you manipulated things to your advantage?"

There's admiration, not accusation, in her words.

"Maybe." I stand very still as she lifts her hand to stroke my cheek.

"You're so much like me. Smart, ambitious, determined … " The fingers trace the length of my nose. "Though you don't really resemble me. Except perhaps about the eyes, and the mouth." She taps her fingers against my lips. "Do you know the main reason I dream of leaving Eco? It's because I want more for you, Ann. More than I had. I hope you know that."

"I know," I reply, although this is the first time I've heard her say it.

She drops her hand to her side. "Eco is such a dead end. What is there for you here, except to keep a greenhouse of plants alive and shack up with that admittedly handsome Asian boy?"

"Raiden Lin."

"Yes, Raiden. Quite a looker. But still, just one more loser who'll never be able to give you what you want, what you deserve."

"Don't think I'd call Raid a loser … "

Mom pats my arm. "Oh, my darling daughter, consider. No plans to leave Eco? Would be perfectly happy screwing you, interspersed with playing holo games and tinkering with those machines your grandfather loves? Yes, I'm afraid 'loser' sums it up quite nicely."

I stare into her lovely face. "I have no plans to shack up with anyone. Not for a while, anyway. Not until we're living on Earth."

My mother's smile turns beatific. "Good girl. You just keep that in mind. Now come, let's head back to our quarters. It's late, and your father will be worried."

As if you care. But I don't speak those words. Like the pathetic chicken-shit I am, I simply smile in return. Like I always do when she's nice to me.

When she shows me a smidgen of love.

Mom drapes her arm about my shoulders as we walk away from the fence. "You and I," she says, as she smoothes my hair with her free hand, "are a force to be reckoned with, Ann Cooper Solano."

I don't bother to correct her version of my name. "The Earth won't know what hit it."

"Not at first, anyway." Mom hugs me closer, forcing me to shorten my stride. "But eventually, everyone will know of our magnificence."

I glance at her face. Her jaw is set, her lips drawn into a thin line. There's no question she's determined to achieve her goals, one way or the other.

With or without me.

I pull the handle of the door that leads into the living quarters and motion for Mom to walk in ahead of me. "Here we are, home sweet home."

She turns in the open doorway to level me with a chilling stare. "This is not home, Ann. Don't forget that. This will never be our home."

I swallow hard and nod in agreement before following her down the hall to our quarters.

***

I can't sleep. Dace's astonished face and Raid's angry one keep swimming before my eyes. There's only one person I want to talk to. I wonder if she's in her room.

It's worth a shot—better than lying here staring at the ceiling. I swing my feet over the edge of my bed, feeling with my toes for the slippers I kicked off earlier. I throw a loose jacket over the T-shirt I wear as a nightgown and slip out of my tiny bedroom—barely large enough to fit a single bed, built-in closet, and dresser—and make my way to our front door. By the variety of snore patterns, I can tell everyone else is asleep.

Emie's family quarters are one hall over. As I pass the door to the rooms where Raid and his mother live, I hesitate. No, I can't talk to Raid now. It's better if he stays angry with me. Perhaps it won't hurt so much when I leave.

The door to Emie's quarters is unlocked—not unusual on Eco. I slip into the living area and tiptoe to Emie's bedroom door, using two knuckles to tap our secret code. I glance about the living area; it looks just like ours, except for the clutter. Emie's mother is less organized than Mom—one reason I always feel more comfortable in this space.

Emie's dark head pokes out from behind the door. "Ann. What's up?"

"Can I come in? Need to talk." I don't wait for an answer. I push past Emie, take a few steps, and flop onto her narrow bed.

"Sure. Make yourself at home." Emie closes the door and stands very still, staring at me.

"So, what was up with you earlier?" I sit up and pat the hard mattress. "Come—talk to me. We haven't talked, *really* talked, in ages."

Emie crosses to the bed. There's a puffiness beneath her dark eyes that tells me she's been crying. "It's the middle of the night."

"We've talked all night plenty of times," I remind her, as she settles beside me.

"Yes, but that was before we had real jobs." Emie uses both hands to smooth down her unruly curls. "You know how demanding Ivana is. She works me to death."

"I know. I lucked out with my grandmother. As long as I get my assigned chores done, she doesn't force me to put in any specific number of hours." I study Emie's face. "You've been crying. Why?"

Emie waves her hand before her face. "Oh, nothing. It's silly. You wouldn't get it, anyway."

"Kam?" She's right; I wouldn't understand shedding any tears over her boyfriend.

"No, nothing to do with Kam, or boys. More important."

"Oh? Spill." I lean back on my elbows and stare at the metal ceiling.

"It's just … " The hesitation in Emie's voice doesn't negate the vibrancy of her tone. "Okay, here's the thing. I chatted with some of the crew of the Augusta Ada this evening. That's why I left the game room early—I wanted a chance to talk to them without … "

"Kam?" I glance over at Emie's solemn face. "So—you arranged a convo with some cybers?"

"Yes. Calla and Jacobi. They were keeping watch over the cargo hold." Emie chews on her pinky nail before continuing. "I saw them earlier in the day and decided I had to speak with them."

"What about?" I sit up and watch Emie closely, a little afraid she's uncovered my lie regarding Captain Patel and his offer.

"Their lives, mostly. How they came to be cybers, what it's like." Emie lays her hand on my arm. "Did you know it can take over twenty operations just to fix one major injury? And they often have multiple injuries. Just imagine how hard it must be."

I recall Calla's artificial face. "I have. It makes me want to puke."

"Think how it makes *them* feel." Emie's tone sharpens. "They are people, not cybers. People with replacement parts, but human just like you and me." Her black eyes flash. "It isn't fair, Ann. They give their all, and what happens? They either spend their lives maimed and crippled or they accept the cyber parts. And once they do, what then? Everyone shuns them. Earth bars them entry. They aren't even allowed to visit their families unless it's off-world."

"That does suck," I admit. "But they knew the dangers when they signed up ... "

Emie continues as if I hadn't spoken. "Did you know that Jacobi has children? Including one he's never seen, except by holo. And Calla has a sister who's very ill. She'll never see her again in person. Neither one of them can hold their loved ones, can even touch their hands. It isn't right, Ann. It just isn't." Tears sparkle on Emie's dark lashes.

"Yes, but what can we do? Not like we have any influence." I frown, realizing I'm not getting any advice out of Emie tonight.

"There must be something." Emie looks me over. "I know we're isolated here, but we do have holo messaging and ships that stop by and all. We could start a protest or maybe some kind of online petition, or … I don't know. But there must be something." She slumps back onto the bed. "I just don't want to be one of those people, like in the holodiscs. Those who witnessed injustice and did nothing."

"Well, you're the computer whiz, or at least you're apprenticed to the guru. You could probably figure out a way to, you know, hack a few sites … "

Emie sits up with a jolt. "Absolutely. Oh, Ann, you're a genius." She pulls me in for a hug.

"Not really," I mutter into her hair. "Emie," I push myself away and peer into her eyes. "Don't do anything stupid. I mean, nothing that will get you in trouble."

"I'm just going to exercise my rights to free speech." There's an expression on Emie's face that worries me. "But, Ann, you came to me for a talk. What's up?"

I shrug. No use going into all that now. "Oh, nothing. Just wanted to share some stuff I learned from Dace. Not really that important."

"Well, I do want to discuss Dace and his scientific interests at some point." Emie smiles. "Must be nice to have another guy crushing on you."

"Dace isn't interested in me," I say, knowing Emie will question this tomorrow when she hears about my kiss. "He's pretty focused on his work—no time for girls."

"Guys our age always have time for girls. Unless they prefer boys, of course." Emie eyes me speculatively. "Maybe that's it?"

"No, I don't think so," I reply, remembering Dace's instinctive response to my kiss. "But like you, he has other things on his mind. By the way," I trace the pattern on her bedspread with one finger. "I suppose I should keep your little convo with the cybers a secret from Kam?"

"If you don't mind."

"I don't. You know how I feel about Kam. Not going to seek him out, at any rate."

Emie plucks at the bedspread. "That's one reason I'm pretty sure Kam and I won't stay together. You know, long-term. Sure, I don't have a gazillion choices, but I think it'd be smarter to live alone than with someone who doesn't believe in the same things I do."

Her expression is pensive. It's okay, I want to say. When I'm gone, you can dump Kam and hook up with Raid— a much better arrangement. I ignore the fluttering in my stomach. I can't be jealous, not when I'm leaving. I'll meet thousands of new people on Earth.

"Don't get me wrong. I enjoy screwing around with Kam. He's pretty damn sexy when he puts his mind to it. But that's all it is, you know. Just some fun."

"Kam might feel differently."

"Maybe." Emie pulls on one of her curls. "You don't think

I'm a bad person, I hope. Leading Kam on and all."

I snort. "No one needs to lead Kam anywhere—he jumps right in, whether he's invited or not. I wouldn't worry about Kameron Frye. When you feel like breaking up with him he'll huff and puff and skulk away—right into the arms of the first under-fifteen who reaches her sixteenth birthday."

"I'm sure." Emie's smile lights up her softly rounded face. "I just want to live my life, you know? I don't want to hurt anyone, but we're so limited here, you have to take your fun where you can. I guess I tend to focus on today, not forever."

Just like Raid. I pat Emie's arm. "Except when it comes to your causes. Never mind, I think you're the best, sweetest person I know. Anyone who says otherwise will have to deal with me."

"Heaven help them," says Emie, her smile broadening. She hugs me again. "Now you'd better head back to your quarters. I do need some sleep. I have to work with Ivana again tomorrow, remember?"

"I know." I tap her gently on the nose. "Sleep well. I'll keep mum about the cybers; trust me." I rise and make my way to the door.

"I always do," Emie calls after me.

I pause with my hand on the latch and almost turn and tell her of the arrangement with Patel. But instead I simply slip out of her room and sneak back to my quarters.

I'll miss Emie. I know she won't abandon Eco—not without her family, and they've never shown any interest in leaving this planet.

Sliding into my bed, I consider a life without Emie. No

Emie, no Raid ... *Stop it*, I command my brain. Don't dwell on that, think of the future. Earth is my goal, my destination, my true calling. I can't allow anything, not even friendship, to stand in my way.

CHAPTER ELEVEN

Dace doesn't race me today—he slows his bike so we ride side by side until we reach the rock pile.

"Ready?" he asks, as we park our bikes and prepare to enter the cavern.

"As I can be," I reply. "One thing, though—if I pass out again, make sure it's not over a sharp rock, okay?"

Dace laughs. I must admit, he has a very nice laugh.

"I promise." He holds out his hand. "Come on, let's see whether our friends are as anxious to greet us as we are to see them."

"Sure they're friends?" I take his hand, noting, not for the first time, that his fingers are cool and dry and stronger than one might expect.

"I just have that feeling," he replies, releasing my hand as we walk into the cavern.

When we reach the lake, Dace busies himself arranging his equipment. "I'm going to set up some new measuring tools."

I lean against the cave wall. "You're really serious about this research, aren't you?"

"Yes." Dace glances over at me. "That's why ... well, I think you're interesting, Ann, and pretty, but I'm not looking for a girlfriend right now."

I watch him focus on adjusting one of his monitors. "And I'm not looking for a new boyfriend. That kiss—I just didn't want you spilling the beans, okay?"

"Okay," replies Dace, without looking up from his busy hands.

"Didn't want you to get the wrong idea."

"I said okay."

The still lake is smooth as a mirror. "Think they'll actually return?"

"Maybe. They seemed as interested in studying us as we were in examining them." Dace finally looks at me. "I just don't want to come between you and your boyfriend, Ann. That's not my thing."

"Good to know." I smile at him. "Don't worry. My plans don't include hooking up with anyone. Not even Raid. I want to get to Earth and figure out my future from there."

Dace fiddles with another monitor. "I hope you won't be disappointed."

This again. "I know all about the problems on Earth. But at least there, I can decide what I want to do. Here, it's all decided for me."

"You mean, you take over your grandmother's work and marry Raid?"

"Yeah," I walk over to him. "That."

"See why you'd feel trapped." Dace moves toward the edge of the lake. "Not sure why so many of your friends seem so complacent, to tell you the truth. Pretty sure I'd feel like you do."

I shrug. "A lot of people on Eco, they figure there's nothing else, so they just work and take their fun where they can find it." I step up beside him, keeping my eyes on the water. "But my mother, she never bought into that philosophy. Always taught me to fight for any opportunity to get back to Earth."

"Pretty obvious that's what she wants." Dace glances at me. "Are you sure it's what *you* want?"

"Yes, I'm sure."

A splash interrupts our conversation. We both stare intently at the lake as the water creature's head breaks the surface.

"Look," says Dace. "There's more than one."

Three more sleek heads pop up. Liquid brown eyes survey us with interest as the creatures bob in the clear water.

Dace's face lights up with joy. "What shall we call them? They need a name."

"I have no clue." I gaze at the creatures. "They probably call themselves something, don't you think?"

"Probably." He turns to me. "Maybe they'll tell you."

I've been bracing myself for a recurrence of the sounds that flattened me yesterday. "Let's not ask."

"Well, I'm going to call them the Selk. After the selkies in Earth folklore."

"Not familiar with that." I make a note to research the term later. "But you can call them whatever you want, I guess. Who's going to argue with you?"

"Hello," Dace says, addressing the creatures. "Do you mind if I call you the Selk?"

Several pairs of bright eyes blink. "Apparently they're not opposed," I observe.

"Oh, did they tell you?" Dace's expression is quite serious.

"No, no. They just seem okay with it, is all."

One of the Selk leaps above the surface and dives under, smooth as sand swept over rock. So they needn't splash. I guess they meant to drench us yesterday.

Dace grabs my forearm. "Can you try to reach out to them? With your mind, I mean. See if you can communicate with them again?"

"Not sure I want to." I purse my lips and stare into the Selks' eyes. "Not fond of passing out."

Dace looks me up and down. "It's a gift."

"In your opinion."

"I wish … " Dace looks away, back toward the water creatures. "I wish I could talk to them." He kneels and reaches out to dip his fingers in the water.

"Careful," I say, as he stretches out his arm.

The Selk swim closer. I crouch down beside Dace and make a grab for his arm. "You're leaning too far … "

He jerks away from me, throwing off his balance and sending him headfirst into the water.

I shriek and fumble for my holofone before remembering

that it'll do me no good inside the cavern. I have no idea if Dace knows how to swim. Worse, it looks like he's knocked his head against the rocky bottom of the lake. That could mean I'll have to jump in and pull him out, and my only experience with swimming is in the virtual world.

Dace's body bobs just below the surface. As I cast about for something to hook his arm and pull him to shore, I notice the Selk circling. *Go away.* I concentrate all my mental energy into this message. *Leave him alone.*

Two of the Selk dive under Dace and position themselves beneath his torso. They rise up, lifting Dace to the surface of the lake. One of the creatures uses its snout to flip Dace over so his face is turned upward, out of the water.

A vivid memory assails me—the Selk's wide mouths, filled with sharp teeth.

Stay away from him!

One of the creatures swims to the shore, right where I'm standing. It rises from the water, keeping itself upright with the steady thrashing of its tail. Staring me straight in the eyes, it extends its small hands. *Air.*

The word reverberates through my head. I swallow hard. *Yes, air. No water.*

The Selk dips its sleek head. It sinks smoothly below the surface and swims to join the other creatures clustered around Dace's dark form.

I suck in a quick breath as I comprehend what's going on. The Selk aren't harming Dace. Two of the creatures are keeping him afloat, balancing him on their backs, while another supports his head with both paws.

In one swift movement, the Selk who confronted me surfaces beside the group and flips Dace on his side.

Dace sputters and spits up water. His eyes widen as he realizes where he is and what's supporting him. He shoots me a look of pure amazement before sliding off the creatures' backs. In the lake, with the Selk surrounding him, he treads water with casual grace.

So he can swim. "You all right?"

"Yes, I think so." He slides one hand over the closest Selk's body. "Can you tell them 'thanks'?"

"Not sure they know what that means." I send the thought anyway.

The Selk move away from Dace, using their tails to propel themselves backward while staying upright in the water. As one, they then leap and dive under the surface and glide toward the opposite side of the lake. Dace watches them for only a second before swimming after them.

"Mierda! Where the hell are you going?" I slap my hand against my thigh. Almost drowns, then swims off with alien creatures? Who does this?

Dace, of course. I sit on the edge of the lake's rocky shore, dangling my feet. I'm ready to slip into the water, armed with a prayer that my virtual lessons have actually prepared me to swim.

But Dace doesn't need my help. His arms cut through the water with the precision of flashing knives. The Selk, swimming underwater, are only shadows. They appear to merge with the far wall and disappear. Reaching the barrier, Dace pauses for only a second before diving beneath the surface.

His dark head pops back up after a moment. "I was right!" He shouts. "There's a passageway beneath the water. Goes right under the wall. Leads to an even bigger cavern beyond this one, it looks like."

"Well, we're not exploring that today," I yell back at him. "Get over here, you idiot. You practically drown and just paddle off like nothing happened."

Dace swims back to me, keeping his head up and parting the water before him with smooth, elegant strokes. "I didn't almost drown. Just got knocked about a bit. I'm actually a very good swimmer."

"Maybe, but you were out cold for a minute." I hold out my hand as he approaches the shore. "You need to have your head examined, and I mean that literally."

Dace laughs. He ignores my hand and, bracing his palms against the rocky edge, pushes his body up and onto the shore. "Freaked you out, did I?" He shakes his head and droplets spray in every direction.

"Gee, thanks." I wipe the water from my face.

"Did you see what the Selk did?" Dace grabs his equipment pouch and fishes out his data recorder. "They saved me, without hesitation."

"I saw." I twitch my lips as Dace starts entering data. "It was pretty awesome."

"Yeah, it was." Dace glances over at me. "Were you going to jump in to rescue me?" He gestures toward my dangling feet.

"Considered it." I pull my knees up to my chest. "You're my

ticket off Eco, don't forget."

"I think maybe you'd do it anyway."

"Maybe. Now, lean over here so I can examine your head. Although," I part his thick hair with my fingers and feel for any bumps, "it is pretty hard. Probably take more than a lake bottom to crack it."

"Hey." Dace winces as I touch a spot near the base of his skull. "Hard heads are actually pretty useful."

"That's what I tell my parents and grandparents. They don't find it amusing either."

Dace lifts his head and my hands fall away. The smile on his face transforms into a very different expression. "You know that thing I said earlier? About not wanting a girlfriend?"

"Hmmm," I murmur, staring into his dark eyes.

"I may have lied."

"You? Hard to believe." I consider sliding back to remove myself from the temptation of his rather luscious lips.

"Honestly, I would love to find a girlfriend. The thing is, when I was younger I spent so much time studying and working to pay for my scientific equipment, I never had time to hang out with anyone, much less girls. So I'm sort of ... behind where people might expect me to be at my age."

"You mean inexperienced."

"Yeah." Dace sighs. "I just worry I'll kiss a girl and she'll think I'm a total idiot. Like, I'll do it all wrong, and she'll never want to see me again."

I choke back a bubble of laughter. "Don't think it would be that drastic, but yeah, could be awkward. So, you want to give it shot and see how you do? I mean, I assume that's what you're asking."

Dace ducks his head. "If you don't mind. I thought you'd be okay with it, since you did kiss me first."

"To shut you up. But sure, give it a try." I concentrate on maintaining a neutral expression.

Dace glances up at me. "You probably think I'm crazy, but you seem so independent, and you already have a boyfriend, and I—well, I just want to avoid complications." He scoots closer to me. "Since I have a plan for my life."

"I have a plan too." It occurs to me that if Connor Patel does honor his word, I will be spending a great deal of time on a crowded spacecraft with Dacian Keeling.

"That's the thing. You're different than most girls I know." He lifts one hand, examining his fingers for a moment before touching my face. "They always seem to want forever right away. Don't think you'd be like that, somehow."

"Not sure I'm good with now, much less forever," I reply, as Dace leans in and searches for my lips.

It's a clumsy attempt—so unlike Raid's smooth, practiced approach. I place one hand behind Dace's head to help guide his effort.

After a few moments Dace sits back on his heels and stares at me.

"Okay?"

"Not bad." I smile. "Just need practice to perfect your technique."

Dace smiles in return, but there's a shadow in his eyes. "I

promise not to ask you again. I just wanted to make sure I wasn't a total loss. Now that I know I'm not, I can think about trying it on some other girls. I mean, kissing you is nice, but I don't want to come between you and your boyfriend. I really hate that shit."

"Never fear." I lean in and give Dace a swift peck on the cheek. "I'm not into the drama. What's a kiss between friends, anyway?"

"So we're friends?

"I guess so." I tap him on the chest, over his heart. "Seems to be the right word."

"I like that word." The color highlighting Dace's cheeks betrays his embarrassment, but I have no intention of mentioning it.

"It's really the best thing, don't you think?" I press my hands against the ground and push myself into a crouch then rise to my feet. "I know it's early, but maybe we should head back? It wouldn't hurt you to rest a bit. You have a definite knot on your head."

"Alright." Dace stares at the hand I've offered him. "I can spend the afternoon analyzing my data. As long as we can come back tomorrow."

"We can, as long as you don't plan to tumble into the lake again."

Dace takes my hand and grips it tightly as I pull him to his feet. "No, I plan to jump in, quite deliberately. Dressed for swimming, and with a waterproof pouch to hold my equipment." He faces me, his gaze unwavering. "I'm going under that wall to explore the next cavern, Ann. With you or without you."

I gaze down my nose at him, hoping to replicate my grandmother's intimidating glare. "I'd better review my holo swim lessons then. 'Cause you sure as hell aren't going without me."

"Don't worry," Dace throws his arm about my shoulders as we move toward the inclined pathway that leads out of the cavern. "I'll keep you afloat."

CHAPTER TWELVE

Arriving back at the compound, I suggest Dace sneak onto the Augusta Ada and change clothes before doing anything else. "Don't want people asking questions. You've mostly dried off, but your jeans are still damp."

"Good point." Dace throws his arm over my shoulders and offers me a quick hug before heading off. "Thanks, Ann, for everything. Same time tomorrow?"

"Sure. And no thanks needed. Just be on time and ready to go."

Dace grins and sketches a mock salute. "At your command, fearless leader."

I wave him away. "Idiot." But I don't try to hide my smile.

"Thanks for everything?" Raid's voice cuts through my thoughts. "What's this 'everything'?"

I turn to face him, freezing the smile on my face as I wonder how much he overheard. "He's just grateful I'm escorting him about. Showing him where to find all the little plants and animals."

"Really?" Raid's eyebrows disappear under his long bangs. "Thought maybe you were sharing more personal discoveries."

"Now, Raid," I conjure my most charming smile, "don't be silly. That kiss in the game room? Nothing but a friendly wager with Emie. She bet me he'd completely flip out."

"Emie wasn't in the room." With his arms crossed over his chest, Raid doesn't look amused.

"I know." I add a little pout. "She won't pay up, either, 'cause she says she didn't see anything. But I won, fair and square."

Raid examines me, his stern expression softening. "I can vouch for you, if it comes to that. Didn't look like Dace was too upset." He drops his arms to his sides.

"Nope. So Emie's conclusion was way off." Dace's kiss in the cavern slips into my mind. "She claims he's a total innocent, but I don't think so."

Raid strokes my cheek with the back of his hand. "Rather cruel, wasn't it? That bet? The poor slob might get the idea you really like him."

"I do like him. Oh, don't make that face. As a friend. He's pretty cool, all in all. You'd like him too, if you'd give him a chance." I lay my head on Raid's shoulder.

"Maybe, but by now he's probably terrified I'll punch him." Raid wraps his arms about me and brushes a kiss across my temple. "A bet? Really, Ann. Poor guy. Why didn't you tell me this last night?"

Because I hadn't thought of it yet. I adjust my smile. "You stormed out so fast, I didn't have a chance. And before I could track you down I had to locate Emie. Who made an early night of it—I found her in her family quarters. Then we started talking …"

"That explains it. You two talking—probably took all night."

"Not quite. But it was late." I allow my body to sink into the warmth of Raid's embrace. Beneath my ear, his heartbeat thumps a steady, reassuring rhythm. "Mmm, you smell nice."

"Flirt. Poor Dace. Poor, poor, Dace." After a moment Raid takes hold of my elbows and forces me to walk backwards until we're standing under the metal overhang of the living quarters' roof.

"What's all this?" I slip out of his hands and bend over to shake the dust from the hem of my jeans.

Raid's fingers light back on my wrist. "Listen, Ann, I know your dream is to leave Eco. But could you consider waiting for a year or two?"

I straighten and tilt my chin to look up into his face. Lacing my words with a teasing tone, I tap his chest with my forefinger and say, "So you can fool around with me for a few more years? Or, at least, until the under-fifteens reach the proper age for seduction?"

Raid doesn't offer his usual slow smile. His dark eyes are shadowed beneath lowered eyelids. It's almost as if he's embarrassed, which is impossible. Raiden Lin, acting nervous in front of a girl? Ridiculous. I stare into his face, trying to decipher the meaning behind his serious expression.

His fingers encircle my left wrist. "So I can figure out how to acquire enough credits to get off this planet." He lifts my hand to his lips. "So we can fulfill that goal together, Ann."

I stare at him, my eyes widening. "What?"

"I have dreams too, you know."

"You never said."

Raid kisses each fingertip on my captured hand before answering. "You never asked." He tilts his head to study my face. "I guess maybe seeing you kiss someone else, I realized how things could change. How I could wake up one day, and you wouldn't be in my life. How we never talk about the future. Or any important stuff, really."

I don't want to discuss this. Not now—not when looking at him just makes me wonder if he carries the same genetic anomaly as I do. Not when I'm about to hide that fact and leave Eco. "Well, this is a shocker. Raiden Lin, serious as death, planning a future with me. Who'd have thought?"

"You should have." Raid presses a kiss into my palm and releases my hand. "But I'll make allowances, since I haven't really been open with you. And I'm sorry about that, Ann. I thought I had all the time in the universe. Last night I realized I was wrong."

I lower my head, embarrassed to meet the honesty in his eyes. Raid, confessing his love for me—it's spun my thoughts about like a sandstorm. It's not something I'm prepared to handle. Not today.

"Raid, I don't know what to say." I take a few steps back and bang into the side of the building. "This is something I'm going to have to think about for a while." I finally steel myself to meet his gaze. "We're still young. I don't know what's gonna happen tomorrow, much less years from now. And I never want to make promises I can't keep."

"I know." All the usual bravado has fled Raid's handsome face, replaced by something I've never seen before—pure, naked emotion. Desire, but not just that. Something more. "But as I told you, I have dreams too. And they all include you. So … just keep that in mind, would you? That's all I ask."

"Sure, I can do that." I curse my cheery tone. *Sure*, I tell him, knowing I plan to abandon him in a week or so. With no goodbye, because of course now there can't be any proper goodbye.

"All I ask." A warm smile illuminates Raid's face.

Maldición. Once a chicken-shit, always a chicken-shit. I smile and turn toward the building door as if nothing's wrong. As if I have no intention of ripping out his heart and tossing it into the trailing flames of the Ada as she, and I, rise off Eco.

"Catch you later," he calls after me.

I duck into the living quarters, mentally planning a day that doesn't involve running into Raid again.

***

As I make my way down the hall, I consider my options. I suppose I can simply hole up in my bedroom and read. Or ask Emie to stop by after work and have another talk. Maybe even drop a hint about my plans. I'm beginning to feel I should prepare her somehow.

I stop short as I reach the entrance to my family quarters. Loud voices roll out from under the door. I can't understand the words, but there's no mistaking the speakers—my mother, father, and grandparents. One less familiar voice breaks through, identifiable by its deep resonance and accent. I can't imagine what Captain Connor Patel is doing in my family quarters at this hour, but it doesn't sound like a friendly visit.

Plastering a smile on my face, I throw open the door and saunter into the living area.

"So you think we should dismantle perfectly good equipment to build some sort of drill?" My grandfather's sitting at the dining table, his back not touching the chair. His black eyes are focused on my mother, who's perched on the edge of the table.

"Yes, Zolin. As I said, this mineral Dacian found is worth the risk. Could make all our fortunes." Mom swings her legs like a child as she faces down the people on the other side of the table.

It's easy to see how the lines are drawn. My grandfather is flanked by my father and grandmother. Connor Patel stands near my mother, close enough to touch her, although he's judiciously clasped his hands behind his back.

"Hello," I say, moving to the middle of the room.

"Ann." My mother slides off the table and hurries over to me. "Come and join us. What we're discussing affects you as much as anyone."

"Discussing?" Grandmother's heavy brows are drawn together. "That's a nice way of putting it."

"Arguing, then," replies my mother with a toss of her shining hair. She grabs me by the hands and pulls me over to the table. "Here, sit down. It'll be good to get a young person's take on this." She shoots my father a sharp glance.

"What's going on?" I meet my grandmother's stern gaze with as innocent an expression as I can muster.

"Your mother," says my grandfather, "wants us to engage in some rather large-scale mining. I've been trying to explain how impractical that could be."

"Because we'd have to raid old equipment for parts?" Mom pulls up a chair and sits beside me. "Equipment we haven't used for years, I might add."

My father sighs and leans forward, his elbows pressed against the table. "But it may still be needed, someday. If the wells run dry … "

"If the wells run dry, if the sky goes dark, if the sun goes nova, if, if, if." Mom examines the perfect ovals of her fingernails. "Honestly, don't you have a shred of imagination left, Jason? This mineral is something that can benefit the entire universe if only we can figure out how to collect enough to make a difference."

"To make a profit, you mean, Tara." My grandmother lays her hand over Dad's tensed arm.

"Well, of course to make a profit. And why not? It could mean enough credits to get all of us off Eco. The children and young people—they could have options for the future Jason and I could only dream of. What's so wrong with that scenario?"

My grandfather leans back in his chair. "The problem is that we don't really have the equipment to do a proper exploration, much less full-scale mining."

Connor Patel unclasps his hands and grips the back of Mom's chair. "But if we could build the necessary tools from old equipment that's just sitting about, we could at least harvest enough of the mineral to convince investors to fund the mining. With every family on Eco guaranteed a cut, of course."

"And you'd get a cut as well, I suppose?" Grandmother looks Patel up and down.

"Well, yes. I'd be offering my assistance to aid the initial mining efforts, as well as conveying samples of the mineral to Earth. We have to show investors the goods, after all."

"We?" My father looks up from the point on the table he's been studying intently. The anger flashing in his dark eyes makes me draw in a sharp breath. "I didn't know you were somehow connected to anything, or anyone, on Eco, Patel."

Time to create a diversion. "What the hel ... heck are you talking about?" I glance about the table. "What mineral?"

Mom turns to me, her hands fluttering like butterfly wings. "Oh, it's miraculous, darling. That piece of rock your friend Dacian ... "

"Dace." I trap Mom's hands between a cage of my fingers and look her directly in the eyes. Her lovely face glows with an unfamiliar expression—joy.

"Dace, then. Anyway, the rock he found is something quite amazing. I unpacked my parents' equipment to examine it, and at first I couldn't believe what I was seeing. So I tested it again and again, but every time the results were the same. Then I knew. We've been handed a miracle."

My grandfather clears his throat, but Mom keeps talking. "Think of it, Ann—a mineral that can clean the air. Clear out impurities, absorb toxins and hold them, keeping humans safe from harm. Can you imagine what that means?"

"It really does that?" My voice squeaks on the last word. I release Mom's fingers. A miracle. I press my knees together to hide their quivering. This could answer all my prayers. Passage off Eco and enough credits to start a successful new life on Earth.

"Apparently." My grandmother's cool voice undercuts my enthusiasm. "Which, as anyone with sense would agree, will prove an extremely valuable resource for deep space exploration and colonization. Not to mention its incalculable benefits to support other terraforming projects. However," Grandmother's tone sharpens, "I question the wisdom of tearing apart our colony's infrastructure in order to exploit this resource."

"Only for a short period of time, Ms. Solano." Patel steps around the table to face my grandmother. "As I explained earlier, I can't just take this one rock to drum up interest. The types of people willing to invest in such a project are going to want at least a few bins full. But I do have room to transport a goodly amount on the Ada, and once we have enough of the mineral to prove the viability of a mining project, entrepreneurs will be fighting each other for the opportunity. You'll have enough credits flowing into Eco to transform this colony into a showplace of modern technology. Not to mention the ability to leave the planet any time you choose."

My father shoves back his chair and jumps to his feet. "There's that 'we' again." He advances until he's toe-to-toe with Connor Patel. His intensity makes him appear taller than he is even though he has to look up to stare into the captain's face. "I'd still like to know what you're getting out of this."

"Connor has offered to broker the deal with some of his contacts." Mom moves to stand beside Patel. Her head only reaches his shoulder, but there's no mistaking who's in charge. Mom turns her laser-bright gaze on my father and his parents.

Dad blinks and audibly swallows. "And you think … Connor can be trusted with this, Tara? No offense, Captain, but we just met you a day or two ago."

"Of course he can be trusted." Mom drapes her slender fingers over Patel's muscular forearm. "Do you think I'm an idiot? I did a little research on the good captain, Jason."

"I'll say." I don't realize I've spoken aloud until five heads swivel in my direction. I cough into my hand. "Sorry, babbling. Long day escorting Dace about and all."

"And of course Dacian … Dace will get a cut of the profits," my mother says, narrowing her eyes as she examines me. "That should more than pay for his university education. No need to worry about a scholarship."

"It could mean a place at a university for Ann as well," adds Patel, with a conciliatory smile for my father.

Dad turns his gaze on Mom. "I understand the benefits. But as my mother has explained, stripping our back-up life-support systems—as you suggested earlier, Captain—hardly seems the smartest tactic."

"We've never used them." Mom steps away from Patel and circles around to stand next to my father. "In all this time, they've never been needed. What makes you think we'd require their use over the next few months?" She touches Dad's arm. "Seriously, my dear, you're being overly cautious."

"Someone needs to be," he replies.

Mom drops her hand, as if burned. "I'd think you'd be willing to consider the opportunity, if only for Ann's sake."

"I am thinking about Ann." My father's eyes focus on Mom's implacable face. "I'm thinking about Ann starving to death because we cannibalized our back-up systems to create your mining machinery. I'm thinking about Ann dying of thirst because our well pumps failed and we had no spare parts to repair them. I'm thinking about all the children and young people on Eco who could suffer if we make bad choices. Expedient, self-serving choices. That's what I'm thinking about, Tara, while you count credits in your head."

"Ann," my mother's voice is silky as the petals of a rose, "why don't you take a nap. You do look exhausted."

Dad smacks his hand against his thigh. "She doesn't have to go anywhere."

My grandparents share a quick glance before Grandfather rises to his feet. "Perhaps it's best if we continue this discussion at another time."

"I'm sorry, Zolin, but this is the only time we have," replies my mother. "I'm taking the information and our proposal to the Governing Council this afternoon so we can call a full colony assembly as soon as possible. You can speak now or wait until the larger meeting."

"You know our opinion." Grandmother stands and moves to Grandfather's side. "We aren't opposed to exploring the possibility of mining sometime in the future. But we don't agree with jumping into something that might jeopardize the colony."

"Well, I told you first as a courtesy. Family, and all that." Mom lifts her chin. "But quite frankly, I don't need your permission to take this to the Council."

Dad shakes his head. "Tara, you need to listen … "

"Damn you—I'm done listening. I've listened to the three of you for far too long. Now I'm going to do the talking, and make some changes around here at last." Mom stalks to the door and yanks it open. "Now's the time for action, not caution." She steps out into the hall without a backward glance.

"Sorry, I didn't mean to cause a fight," says Patel.

"You didn't," replies my father. "It started long before you landed on Eco." He crosses to the table and slumps into a chair.

Patel runs his hands through his hair as his gaze darts about, landing on everything except the faces of the three people standing before him. "Excuse me, please. Matters on the Ada demand my attention." He strides out of our quarters, allowing the door to slam behind him.

My grandfather takes a seat next to my dad. "We'd better pull up some equipment plans, son. Best to be prepared for whatever the Council and the colony decide."

"Anna-Maria," Grandmother levels one of her piercing stares at me, "come along. We've work to do in the greenhouse, if you're done escorting Dace for the day."

I'm more than happy to leave this room. "No problem," I reply.

I spare one glance, and a smile, for my father before I follow her into the hall.

CHAPTER THIRTEEN

I wait until we're in the cavern to inform Dace of my mother's plans.

"She can't do that!" Dace rakes his fingers through his hair, causing it to stand up in spikes.

Sitting on one of the larger boulders, I pull off my boots. "Unfortunately, she can."

"You have to stop her." Dace has already stripped down to a pair of shorts. A waterproof pack is strapped about his waist.

I yank off my socks and study my bare toes. "Can't. She's on the governing council and has every right to bring this to their attention. In fact, she already has. Informed them yesterday, from what I heard."

"And you're just telling me now?" Dace sits at the edge of lake, dangling his legs in the water.

"Wouldn't have made any difference." I pile my clothes, boots and other gear behind the boulder. I'm wearing a tank top and a pair of shorts, the darkest I could find. They might cling to my skin, but at least they shouldn't turn transparent.

"If they decide to mine this cavern, even on a small scale, it could be disastrous for the Selk." Dace's lower lip rolls into its accustomed pout as he stares over the still lake.

I sit next to him. "Maybe the colony will vote it down."

"You don't believe that." Dace shakes off the hand I've laid over his wrist. "And you're probably all for the mining, anyway. Then your family can leave Eco any time they choose, and with a pile of credits."

"My mom said she'd make sure you got your cut."

"Yeah, great." Dace turns to me, his dark eyes brimming with suspicion. "You didn't happen to mention the Selk, I suppose? No, judging by that guilty look, I guess not. So the council and colony have no idea they'll be damaging a native life form. Way to go, Ann. Letting them vote without knowing all the facts. Classy."

"Now, look here, Dacian Keeling." I slide away from him. "You promised you wouldn't mention these creatures, or any genetic connections to them, until we're both safely off Eco. Are you going to keep that promise?"

Dace returns my stare with a glare of his own. "Maybe. If you promise to somehow convince your mother and the others to drop their plan to mine the caverns until we devise a way to move the Selk. Maybe you can at least communicate the danger to them before you get the hell off Eco."

"What good's that going to do? If the mining starts, do you really think they won't strip the planet bare? Face it, Dace—the Selk are pretty much doomed." I dip my toes in the water. It's strange how this thought makes my chest tighten. I don't know why. Whatever happens, I won't be around to witness it.

"No, they're not. Not if I have anything to do with it. There's an entire maze of caverns, I expect. If we could get the Selk to travel to another area of the planet, far from the compound, they might be safe for a while." He drops his head and breaks our staring match. "Until I can get help."

"What kind of help?"

Dace plucks at the strap of his pack. "I know people."

"Greeners, you mean?" I give the rubber band holding my braid a final twist. "Just what we need—a bunch of crazy eco-terrorists crawling all over the planet."

"They aren't terrorists." Dace avoids my eyes as he slips into the water. "That's just 'sphere propaganda." Hanging onto the rocky edge, he finally glances up at me. "You are going to talk to your mom, right? Even if she's already told everyone about the mineral, she might still be able to convince them to hold off on the mining."

"I'll talk to her." This will do no good, of course, but promises are easy to make.

Not so easy to keep. I shake my head and kneel into a crouch, gripping the stones that line the edge of the lake. Without another thought, I lower myself into the water.

Dace's hand slaps down over mine. "Hang on. You said the only swimming you've ever done was in a simulation."

"True." It's strange to be immersed in water. I've taken showers all my life—there's no such thing as a bathtub, much less a pool, on Eco. I kick my feet underwater and marvel at the lack of resistance. "I was pretty good, though."

"In a holo-game." Dace pries one set of my fingers off the ledge. "Hold onto my hand, close your eyes, and keep kicking. Just like you did in the holo. Yeah, treading water, there you go. Now, drop your other hand and move it through the water, like you're making a small circle."

Eyes closed, I grip his fingers like a vise as he pulls me around until my back is brushing the rocks. The water's just warm enough to be comfortable. It's smooth as silk gliding over my skin. I slow my feet until I'm kicking rhythmically rather than thrashing.

"Super." Dace wiggles his fingers to loosen my hold on his hand.

The water feels good. Right. I'm weightless as a spacer in zero-grav. I'm floating in the clear sky. I'm home.

My eyes fly open when Dace slides his hand away.

"Circles with the free hand too," he says. "Look at you—doing great!"

I bob in the water, held up by its buoyancy and the slow movements of my hands and feet. Above my head the silver flakes in the dark rock twinkle like stars.

"You're a natural!" Dace swims in a circle around me. "It's like you were born to it." He pauses, treading water in front of me. His eyes narrow. "Like it's in your bones."

"Don't go all scientific on me." I sweep my arms in wider circles, imitating the movements I learned in the holo-game. I recall a frog-like motion that could replace the straight kicks of my feet. Knees up and out and glide.

"Damn." Dace swims up beside me. "Never saw anyone learn that fast."

I flip my braid over my shoulder, showering Dace with a spray of droplets. "It was all that holo practice."

"Was it?" Dace shoots a sharp glance my way. "Nothing to do with that little DNA string then?"

"Of course not." I fight the urge to dive under the surface. It feels like the natural thing to do, but I'm certainly not that experienced at swimming yet. Still …

I dive, propelling my body through the water until I reach the middle of the lake. Surfacing, I draw in a deep gulp of air.

"Holy shit, Ann." Dace bobs up beside me. "You're half fish."

I slap the water in front of me, splashing a small wave into his face. "Don't say that!" I turn and swim for the far wall.

"Sorry." Dace shouts, keeping pace with my fierce strokes.

I swim faster.

When we reach the far wall we both grab for a protruding chunk of rock at the same time. Our hands collide. Before I can pull away, Dace clutches my fingers and holds tight. "I really am sorry. That was crappy of me."

I catch my breath before replying. "It was. And untrue, no matter how you look at it. You said yourself the Selk are mammals, not fish."

Dace stares into my eyes for a moment before his contrite expression dissolves into a smile. "Yeah, definitely not fish." He squeezes my hand. "I think maybe you are a brand new species, though. You're sure not like any other girl I've known."

I can't stay angry in the presence of that smile. "Well, that means squat. You've confessed your limited experience with girls." Dace laughs. "Okay, okay. Point taken." He lifts his hand off mine and his dark eyes rake over my face. "One thing's for sure, though, you're like a new discovery every day. I never know what you're going to say or do next. I may not know much about girls, but I know you're special, Ann Solano."

"Dive," I reply.

We submerge and swim through the wide passage that leads under and beyond the wall.

Surfacing on the other side, I tread water as I face at least ten of the Selk. "Hello." I speak aloud first, before sending the thought. *Hello.*

Air. Water.

I nod my head at them and gaze about. Yes, lots of air and water. We're in a much larger cavern, with a ceiling so high the airshafts are nearly invisible. But I spy slivers of sky threading the dark stone like a web of white fire. The silver flakes caught up in the stone sparkle in the light reflected back from the water. Around this lake is a shoreline of stone. Clusters of the Selk rest upon the rocky ledges.

All the alien eyes are fastened on Dace and me, but only the few Selk in the lake move, swimming toward us.

"They live out of the water, too." Dace's voice is hushed.

"Apparently."

In a far corner floats a patch of emerald leaves, large and flat as plates. Fragile stems rise from the leaves, swaying under the weight of golden, bell-like flowers. Beautiful and strange, and undoubtedly the source of the traces of vegetation Dace found a few days ago.

The Selk welcome party encircles us as we continue to tread water.

"Do they understand hello?" Dace moves closer to me.

"Not sure." I concentrate on sending positive messages. *Friends. Hello. We are friends.*

One of the Selk slides up next to me. Its fur is sleek and damp, but surprisingly warm. I lift one hand and allow my fingers to hover over its back. I want to touch it, but I don't.

Before I can pull my hand away, the Selk rises up, pressing its body against my palm.

Us.

I lose all my buoyancy, falling back with a great splash. My head slaps the surface and water rushes up my nose. My extremities tingle as if stung by thousands of insects.

Dace grabs my arm to yank me back to the surface. "You okay?" His eyes are filled with concern.

As are the eyes of the Selk. It leans in and butts my chest with its snout. *Air. Breathe.*

"I am breathing." From Dace's puzzled expression I assume I'm speaking aloud. *Yes, breathing.*

The Selk swims under my right arm. The warmth of the creature radiates through my bones, and I'm veiled in a calm that slows my rapid breathing. I lean into the slick, furry bulk of the Selk's body, allowing my arm to drape across its back.

You. Thank you. I push the thoughts forward.

The Selk rolls over on its side, until its dark eyes are fixed on mine. *Us.*

I shake my head. *Not us. Me. You. Different.* I tap my chest. *Human.*

"Are you talking to them?" Dace swims around to the other side of the Selk.

"Yes. It keeps saying 'us.' I was trying to explain that we're different."

"Maybe not so very, in their eyes."

I meet Dace's serious gaze over the Selk's back. "I don't know if that's what they mean."

"You don't know it's not."

"No, I … "

The Selk shoots out from under my arm like a torpedo, gliding toward the far shore. In the middle of the lake it turns to gaze at us, lifting one of its small paws.

"I think it wants us to follow," observes Dace.

"Really, genius? You think so?" I swim away from him, toward the Selk.

As I approach, the creature leaps up, arcing its body above the surface before diving under. I follow its swift-moving silhouette, Dace close behind me. When we reach the opposite shore the Selk surfaces and slides onto a natural ramp of rock, propelling its bulky body clear of the water.

I climb the ramp on my hands and knees. Reaching the top of the incline, I pull myself into a sitting position. Dace flops beside me with a grunt.

"Must've sensed we needed a rest." Dace eyes the Selk as it

maneuvers its flipper tail so it's curled around the base of its torso, creating a natural support for its upper body.

Other Selk lounge all around us—some even bulkier than the creature that guided us across the lake. A few are considerably smaller, but from the way they're huddled next to larger creatures, I assume the little ones must be babies. Our Selk companion barks once and all the brown heads swivel in unison to study us with dark, limpid eyes.

"This," says Dace, staring at the clusters of alien creatures, "could be dangerous."

I lay my hand on his knee. "I don't think they plan to harm us."

Dace's gaze shifts to me. "They told you?"

"No. They don't really speak—sorry, I guess 'think' is the better word—in complete sentences. I get these fragments. More like ideas, but they're very basic concepts. Nothing as elaborate as language."

"It's communication."

"Yeah, I guess it is."

We sit in silence, examining the Selk as they examine us.

After several minutes, the Selk that greeted me in the water waddles toward a dark patch in the cavern wall. It turns its head to stare back at us.

Dace scrambles to his feet. "I think it wants us to follow again."

"Seems like it." I rise and trail after Dace as he threads his way through the clusters of creatures. The scent of damp fur assails my nostrils, and I press my hand beneath my nose to block the smell. "Looks like we're heading for a dead end, though."

"Nope." Dace disappears from view, and I realize what I took for a solid wall is a short section that blends into the blackness of the surrounding stone.

I slip behind the panel of rock and into another passageway. A narrow path runs along one wall, bordering a body of water as straight as a man-made canal. "So your theory's correct—it's all connected."

Dace shoots a grin at me over his shoulder. "Despite your obvious doubt, I am occasionally right."

Our Selk guide rises up, balancing on its flipper, and dives into the canal. Its awkward waddle is transformed into sleek symmetry as it swims toward a sliver of light.

Dace and I increase our strides, reaching the point where the passage makes a sharp turn to the right. The Selk has already vanished around the corner as we stumble, blinking, into another chamber.

This one is small but open to the sky. The Selk stops swimming and bobs in the pool of water, which is clogged with more of the flat-leafed plants as well as other vegetation. *Light. Air.*

And food? I kneel beside the water and touch the curling tendril of one of the plants. It's purple as a ripe eggplant.

Dark brown eyes regard me with interest. The Selk plucks a piece of the floating vegetation with one paw. Lifting it to its snout, it takes a quick bite. *Eat.*

"Amazing." Dace whips out one of his monitors and holds it out before him. "Can you grab me a piece of that stuff, Ann?"

I break off a bit of the vine. "Sure. Seems to be what our

friend wants, anyway." I snap the tendril in half and hand Dace a piece while I sniff the other portion. "Smells like green beans."

"But with much more protein." Dace inserts the piece of alien vegetation into a Lucite vial and tucks the tube and his monitor into the pouch strapped to his waist. "The colonists never discovered this? I would've thought your grandmother might have searched it out long ago, being a botanist and all."

"She doesn't come out into the wild." As soon as the words leave my mouth, my mind wrestles with this truth. I've always considered my grandmother fearless, but the fact she's never, to my knowledge, discovered these native botanical wonders makes me question this belief. "They weren't sent here for exploration, you know."

Dace shrugs. "I suppose not. But I bet she'll find this fascinating."

I jump to my feet. "We can't tell them yet. Remember?" I wipe my dripping hands on my equally damp shorts as I eye Dace with suspicion.

"I thought maybe you'd change your mind about that." Dace meets my gaze without flinching. "Considering what your mom and my uncle are up to. If they knew about these creatures and your connection to them ... "

"No way." My tone's obviously troubling the Selk. It swims closer to the shore, chattering a string of squeaks. *Okay*, I think, although that's probably not a concept it can understand. *Good.*

"They need to know, Ann. If they have all the facts, I'm sure they won't bring in machines to wreck the Selk's habitat."

"I'll talk to my mother. I'll find a way to stall them." My nails dig into my palms. "Just don't say anything. Or … " I fix Dace with an icy glare. "I'll never bring you back here. You know your uncle won't let you go outside the compound unescorted."

"I could sneak out." Dace's gaze doesn't waver.

"You could. But I could plant a little bug in your uncle's ear, mention hidden dangers and how I feel we shouldn't continue exploring. I bet he'll lock you in your berth until you leave this planet."

We face each other, both breathing hard. The Selk sings out a long trill of ringing tones. "Maldición!" I clutch at my ears. The reverberation is rattling my thoughts.

"Truce," says Dace, with a quick glance at the water creature. "Let's just work together, okay?"

I nod as the ringing fades away. "Deal."

"There's actually a way to the surface." Dace points toward a jagged path that leads upward. "Funny, that."

"The paths?"

"Yes. Almost look like they aren't natural, only … " Dace shakes his head. "Don't think the Selk could carve out something like that."

"No." I contemplate the implications of this thought as I stare into the Selk's face. "How 'bout we head back to our bikes? We have to make that swim again before we're too exhausted."

Dace looks over at me, his dark eyes shadowed beneath his thick lashes. "I think you could swim it in your sleep."

"Don't give me that half-fish crap again. I just have some natural ability, that's all." I twist the band one more time around the bottom of my braid. It snaps and my hair springs free. "Now look what you've done."

Dace cocks one eyebrow. "Me? My hands were nowhere near you."

"You and your weird genetic ideas—always making me nervous." I comb my fingers through my hair. "It's going to be all up in my face while we're swimming."

Dace fishes around in his equipment pouch. "Here." He tosses me a coil of elastic. "Always keep some lastic-rope on me. Comes in handy."

"You stashed a whole laboratory in there?" I eye Dace as I wrap the springy rope about my hair, tying it off to create an impromptu ponytail.

"Pretty much." He waves at the Selk. "Goodbye for now, and thank you."

The creature cocks its head and examines Dace.

"It likes you, I think." I move toward the dark passage that leads underground. *Friend.* I wave my hand in Dace's direction.

Friend. The Selk propels itself backward in the vegetation-clogged pool. It dives under the surface and disappears—headed, I imagine, back to its colony.

Dace and I navigate the dark passage without conversation. When we reach the lake, I note that most of the Selk have disappeared from the ledges. Several dark heads bob in the water, but not enough to account for all the creatures. "That's odd. I didn't see any of them in the canal, except for the one guiding us."

Dace stretches his arms above his lean body. "Probably other underwater passages leading to who-knows-where. More to explore another day." His face lights up in anticipation.

"But not today." I sit down on the smooth ramp and use my hands to propel my body into the water. "Come along, we've experienced more than enough adventure for now."

Dace slips by me, sliding down the ramp headfirst. Surfacing, he splashes water over my bare shoulders. "There's never enough adventure. Ouch, if looks could kill … " He grins. "Okay, show the way, fearless leader."

I snort and give a strong frog kick to glide away from him. "You are so full of shit, Dacian Keeling."

"Could be." Dace swims up alongside me. "But it's interesting shit."

I laugh, swallowing a mouthful of water. Lifting my head, I expel the liquid—in Dace's direction.

He dives too quickly to be hit. I follow him under the wall that separates the two caverns, and when we clear the wall I make a grab for one of his fluttering feet.

He rolls as my fingers close over his ankle. He shakes off my grip and leans in to place his hands about my waist. Entwined, we kick and shoot upward, breaking the surface.

"Let go!" I fling my head, whipping my ponytail into Dace's face.

He sputters and throws up one hand to brush the wet strands away. His other hand locks firmly to my waist. "Your attempt to capture me failed. Now I've got you. Admit defeat."

"Never." I use one hand to slap a tiny tsunami of water into his face.

Dace shakes his head and leans in, pressing his forehead

against mine. "Not so fast, fish girl."

His eyes are fixed on mine, inches from my face, mesmerizing as the heart of an unfolding flower. Layers upon layers.

I tuck my chin to my chest. "I told you not to call me that, science geek."

"But I like fish. They are infinitely interesting." Dace's full lips slide down my damp cheek and land on my mouth.

The lake laps against my skin, feet flutter, the feel of Dace's lips on mine as we bob in the silky water.

Dace pulls away first. "Didn't plan that."

"You're not supposed to." I tap his nose with one finger. "Lesson number two in my kissing girls course, free of charge."

Dace's lips twitch. "Thanks, I think. Now—race me to the shore, mermaid."

He releases me and turns a somersault under water. Swearing, I follow, kicking as hard as I can to keep up with his fierce strokes. We reach the ragged shoreline at almost the same moment. We hoist our slippery bodies onto the rocky ledge.

"What a great idea," I pant. "Talk about exhaustion. And we still have to climb out of here, you idiot." I wave my hand toward the path.

"Oh," says Dace, in quite a different voice.

I follow his gaze to the bottom of the inclined ramp.

Raid is standing there.

CHAPTER FOURTEEN

R aid says nothing, merely saunters toward us, exaggerating his customary swagger.

"How'd you find us?" I jump to my feet as Raid moves closer. We're toe to toe. I stiffen my back. Might as well meet that sneer with bravado.

"Followed the tracks. Saw your bikes parked outside and boot prints leading to an opening in the rocks. Figured it out fairly quickly." Raid's eyes narrow, slicing his face like razor blades. "May not be as clever as the professor here, but I do possess a few brain cells."

Dace rises to his feet. "Don't get the wrong idea." He sweeps up our discarded clothes. "We've just been exploring."

"Obviously." Raid shoots a fierce glare my way before gazing around the cavern. "What's this place, anyway? Besides your personal playground, I mean."

"Part of an interconnected cavern system that runs beneath the surface of Eco." Dace refuses to take the bait. He moves closer, dropping the clothes at his feet.

Raid looks me over. "Interesting outfit. Been swimming? Didn't know you had it in you, Solano."

"You don't know everything about me." I pluck at the edge of my tank top. My wet top and shorts cling to my curves like a second skin.

Raid's expression changes. The anger morphs into something else, something that sends a flush radiating out from the nape of my neck. I cross my arms and hug my body.

Raid flexes his fingers before shoving his hands into his pockets. "Learning more all the time."

Fabric drapes over my bare skin. I turn my head. Dace is standing behind me, adjusting my jacket around my shoulders.

"Anyway … " Dace steps back. He grabs his T-shirt and continues to talk while he slides it over his head. "We suspect Eco's laced with a network of underground lakes and rivers, all linked together." Pulling down the shirt to cover his slender torso, Dace eyes Raid without rancor. "Something you might have found sooner if you'd bothered to, you know, explore the planet you live on."

Raid yanks his hands out of his pockets. The fingers are balled into fists. "Think you're pretty clever, don't you, spacer? Well, in case you hadn't noticed, some of us have to work. Don't have the luxury of farting around all day."

"It's not play." I lift my chin so I can stare into his face. "Dace's research is every bit as important as your job, Raiden Lin. And I've been his guide, not some follower."

Raid taps my lips with two fingers. "No doubt. Seems like you've been teaching him quite a few things."

I swat away Raid's hand. "Who says I had to teach him anything?"

I catch the flash of a smile before Dace ducks his head and concentrates on pulling on his pants.

"So, thought you'd experiment a bit before spacer here blasts off for parts unknown?" There's a flicker of pain in Raid's eyes.

"Honestly, Raid," I grab one of his fists and pull it to my chest, "is that all you think of me? Just some girl making out with any guy she can get her hands on? I thought you knew me better than that."

"So did I." Raid unclenches his hand under the caress of my fingers. "But I did see the kissing, Ann. More than once. Don't think you can pass it off as a bet this time."

Dace fishes through the pile of clothes at his feet. "Ann might be blasting off with us, you know." He tosses my jeans at me. "And—what bet?"

"Never mind. Isn't important." I shoot Dace a warning look. Turning my attention back to Raid, I toss my hair and lift our entwined fingers to my lips. "Kisses are fun. But I'm not looking for something more right now. You should know that better than anyone, Raid." I press a kiss into his palm and drop his hand. "And when I am, it'll be me that decides, not any boy. You got that?"

Raid examines me with great deliberation. After a moment a

smile curves his lips. He reaches out to smooth down my unruly hair. "Got it."

"So, might as well chill, dude." Dace sits on one of the scattered boulders and tugs on his socks. "Ann hasn't sworn her eternal love or anything. We've really been concentrating on the research. And, news flash—we've discovered some amazing things down here. Pretty major stuff."

To my surprise, Raid looks at Dace with admiration. "Yeah? Well, I've already heard about the mineral that's going to make us all rich." Raid's lips twitch. "Promissium, your mom's calling it."

"You must be joking."

"No. Kind of stupid, but the others are already throwing around the term like it's some magic spell. Like it's going to change everything."

"So they're going along with Ms. Solano and her mining plans?" Dace glances up from his boots, his expression darkening.

"Cooper," I reply automatically. "Tara Cooper. She never took my dad's name." I slide past Raid and scoop up the rest of my clothes. "Stupid tradition anyway."

Raid nods. "One of those independent types. Like mother, like daughter."

"And proud of it." I wobble on one foot and then the other, aware of Raid's scrutiny as I work my jeans up my damp legs. "So—the colonists agree with Mom? We're going to mine the crap out of Eco?"

"Maybe. Your grandparents are opposed. And a few others."

"My father?"

"Goes back and forth." Raid steps forward to offer me his

bent elbow. I meet his sardonic grin with a frown as I balance against his arm.

"And the kids?" I pull on my socks.

Raid shrugs. "Not really decided. Wait, that's the wrong foot."

"I'm aware," I snap, making the switch with my boots.

Dace stands and strides over to us. "We need to get back. As soon as possible. Ann needs to talk to her mother about delaying the mining."

"Ann? Talk to her mother?" Raid's grin broadens. "That'll be interesting."

"Interesting or not, it needs to happen." Dace's gaze never leaves my face.

"It will." I let go of Raid's arm and press my toes down into my boots. "I'll corner her as soon as we get back. As soon as I can trap her alone, that is."

"What the hell is that?" asks Raid, peering over my shoulder.

Dace and I turn as one, just in time to see a sleek brown head lift above the surface of the water.

Raid moves to the edge of the lake as if drawn by a tractor beam. The Selk swims closer to shore and rises up before him. Its dark eyes scan his face for a full minute before it emits a trill of sounds.

Dace and I dash forward to catch Raid as he stumbles and falls.

"Shit! Make it stop!" He claps his hands over his ears.

The sounds ring in my head as well, but I allow them to ripple through my body without fighting the sensation. *Hello. Friend. Good.*

I tap Raid's leg. *Yes, friend. But sound hurts.*

The Selk cocks its head to the side. *No hurt.* It snaps its mouth shut.

As the reverberation falls away, Raid slumps back on his heels and stares at the water creature. "It said 'friend.' I mean," he shakes his head, "it didn't say that, but that was the idea in my head, somehow … "

"Yes, they can communicate with us, to a certain degree. Conceptually, anyway." I grab one of Raid's arms as Dace grips the other and we help him to his feet. "I hear it too."

Raid looks down into my face. "But it didn't affect you."

"Not anymore. It did at first. What you have to do," I reach up to sweep the fall of dark hair out of his eyes, "is allow the ideas to just roll over you. Don't focus on the sounds."

Raid traps my falling fingers between his palms. "So how long have you known about these … creatures?"

"Not long. Dace and I encountered them a few days ago. We call them the Selk."

"And what are they?"

"Don't know exactly," Dace says. "Mammals, for sure. They breathe air but live primarily in water. I mean, they're an alien species. I haven't worked up all the biological info yet." Dace fiddles with the closure on his equipment pouch. "I'll know more when I can run a full panel of tests."

Raid stares back into eyes of the Selk. "It isn't frightened."

I focus on Raid's face. There's a look of wonder in his eyes—a childlike gleam I've never seen before. "No, not at all. Of course, humans have never caused the creatures any harm."

"Yet," says Dace.

"Are there a lot of them down here?" Raid lifts one hand and holds it before the Selk's snout.

"Quite a few. We saw at least forty in the adjacent cavern. Many more spread throughout the underground waterways, I expect." Dace smiles as Raid flexes his fingers. "Go ahead, it won't bite."

Before Raid can stretch out his hand the Selk pushes its snout into his open palm. Raid stands transfixed as the creature rubs against his fingers.

I jab Raid's arm with my elbow. "Wow, it really likes you. I didn't get that warm a welcome the first time."

"What does it mean, 'us'?" Raid turns to me, his eyes bright as stars. "I keep hearing 'us.'"

I duck my head, ashamed to meet his brilliant gaze. "I don't know. I've heard that too. Talking about the entire group of Selk, maybe?"

Dace coughs, loudly.

"So, about that getting back … " I tug on the sleeve of Raid's shirt.

Raid gives the Selk a final pat before stepping back from the edge. "This mining," he turns his face toward Dace, "it will destroy these creatures? Or at least their home?"

"Probably."

The Selk barks once. Arching its neck, it dives directly down into the water. Its bulky form somersaults with the grace of a falling leaf before it levels out and speeds away toward the opposite wall.

"Where'd it go?" Raid rubs his neck with one hand and stares across the lake.

"There's a passage under the wall." I take Raid's arm. "Let's go now, okay? And Raid—don't say anything about these creatures to anyone else yet."

"Why?" Raid shudders, as if emerging from a trance. His eyes narrow and focus on me. "Why shouldn't I say anything, Ann?"

Why shouldn't he? I glance over at Dace, who simply shrugs his shoulders. "It might affect Dace's research. Too many people tromping down here to see the Selk—could taint the results."

Dace coughs again. "Yeah, that could happen," he says, as Raid shoots him a suspicious look.

"I'd hate to think we'd kill off all these creatures." There's a wistful note in Raid's voice.

I study his profile. I've known him all my life, yet question what other layers of his personality have remained hidden from me. Because he's buried them? Or because I never bothered to look beyond the surface of his handsome face? "Sorry," I say under my breath. Raid glances down at me with a question in his dark eyes. "Sorry we ever discovered them, if that's the case."

"That would be a pity." Raid shakes out his arms. "Weird, the way it made me feel. Like I just wanted to press my hands into its fur and never let go."

Dace's speculative stare is leveled on Raid. "They are lovely creatures. Well, maybe not beautiful in the traditional sense, but they seem to radiate warmth and intelligence. Such … oh, I don't know."

"Joy," says Raid. "Such joy."

I fight the desire to wrap my arms around him. "Well, if we're gonna convince Mom and the others to hold off their mining plans, we'd better get to it."

I shove the rest of my clothes into my pack as Dace double-checks his equipment pouch. Raid continues to stare moodily across the lake. When I head for the path out of the cavern, the others follow without a word. Only when we step outside, blinking in the sunlight, does anyone speak again.

"Us," says Raid, as he straddles his bike. "Just wish I knew what that 'us' really meant."

I slam down my visor and rev up my bike to avoid a reply.

CHAPTER FIFTEEN

We approach the compound. Dace rolls up beside me and shouts that he's heading for the back gate, near the ship. I nod and motion for Raid to follow.

We park the bikes in the shadow of the spacecraft's tailfin. As I yank off my helmet, loud voices waft from the cargo hold.

"What the hell?" Dace tosses his helmet over his handlebars and jogs toward the source of the noise.

Raid and I stride after him. When we reach the open doors of the hold, I spy a dark head and a golden one poking out above a wall of crates. Facing them is another figure, with hair the color of flame.

"You shouldn't mess with these creatures," says Kam. "You're getting all screwed up, Emie."

Dace charges up the loading ramp. "What's going on here?"

I follow Raid as he steps around the barrier of boxes. Emie and Calla are standing side-by-side, confronting Kam, whose fingers are clenching and unclenching at his sides.

"Just trying to convince my girlfriend she's got better things to do than waste hours yapping with cybers." Kam's eyes glitter like the scales of a snake.

"Convince? Sounds like orders to me." Dace steps between Kam and the two women. "Shouting doesn't do much to convince anyone of anything."

If Kam's eyes were lasers, Dace would be dead. "Not your biz, spacer. Just walk away."

"Hey now." Raid slides behind Kam and lays a hand on his shoulder. "Chill out, dude. Looks like Emie was just chatting. Where's the harm?"

"The harm?" Kam shrugs off Raid's hand. "The harm is she's spending all her free time with this trash when we've made prior plans. And even when we're together, all she talks about is the injustice of the genetic laws and how badly cybers are treated and blah, blah, blah." He curls his lip as his gaze turns to me. "It's you, isn't it, Solano? Putting ideas in her head."

I move to stand beside Emie. "No, it isn't. For your information, Kameron Frye, Emie has plenty of her own ideas in her head. Her brain isn't empty, you know. She doesn't need me to place anything there."

Emie's fingers creep into my palm. "Damn straight, Kam. I do actually have a mind of my own." She glances up at me with a faint smile and gives my hand a squeeze.

I smile in return before turning my attention back to Kam.

"Emie's probably smarter than me, if it comes down to it. So stop treating her like she's your robot."

"Look, dude, whatcha say we fire off some rounds of laser-blast," says Raid. His tone is light, but his expression, glimpsed over Kam's shoulder, is grave. "Need another chance to whoop your ass, power jockey."

"Not until this cyber promises to leave Emie alone."

Calla's artificial face displays no emotion, but something dangerous flickers in her eyes. "I don't seek her out. She comes to talk with me." She takes a step toward Kam. "It seems Emie's interested in more than your little world can offer."

Dace puts out a hand to halt Calla's forward momentum. "Not the place for an argument. My uncle won't be happy if we destroy his property."

Calla stares at Dace for a moment before her lips ratchet into a semblance of a smile. She pats Dace's arm. "Good point, little man. The captain will have my hide if we damage any of this." She jerks her head to indicate the crates piled about the cargo hold.

"Well, I don't give spacer's shit about that." Kam shoves Dace aside to confront Calla. "I don't much care for your captain either when it comes down to it."

Calla's gaze sweeps over Kam. "You really don't want to piss me off, dirt-treader." Her hand slides down to the laser gun holstered at her side.

Dace leaps in between them. "No violence. That never solves anything."

The boy has guts. Glancing at Raid, I note my admiration

mirrored in his eyes. "This is ridiculous." I grip Emie's hand with so much force she squeaks.

Raid leans in and grabs Kam by the upper arm. "Time to go. Last thing we need is to be forced to pay for damaged property."

"You're all assholes!" Kam struggles against Raid's hold, but he's not strong enough to dislodge Raid's fingers. "Bleeding-heart idiots—you don't see the danger right in front of your snotty noses."

"And what danger is that?" asks Emie, pulling her hand from mine. She steps up beside Calla. "What're you so afraid of, Kam?"

"Not afraid—disgusted." Kam spits at Calla's feet.

The cyber's fingers twitch over her gun. "Nah, dirt-treader, 'afraid' is the right word. You're scared shitless 'cause you know one wrong move, one false step on your turbine platform, and you could be me." She stares directly into Kam's eyes. "Any one of you could be me. That's why you hate cybers so much."

"Abomination!" Kam lurches forward, but Raid throws his arms around the redhead to hold him in place.

"Enough." Raid tightens his hold and backs away, dragging Kam with him. "You've lost your tiny mind. I'm carting you out of here until you cool off."

"Joining up with the mutant brigade, are you, Raid?" Kam twists his neck to send Raid a furious sidelong glance. "Guess it's 'cause you love crazy-bitch Solano over there." He spits again, hitting Raid's boot.

"I do love her," says Raid, with perfect conviction.

I meet his calm gaze. Out of the corner of my eye I notice Dace's focus shift from Kam to Raid.

"But that's got nothing to do with me stopping you from doing something majorly stupid." Raid releases Kam for a second before yanking his arms behind his back. "Now, we're going to march out of here, and you're going to show me where to scrounge up some booze from your uncle's not-so-secret still. 'Cause you need a drink, Kam, and then—if you still feel like making trouble—you and I can engage in some holo game anarchy."

"Emie, stay with that creature now and we're done! Don't come running after me later!" shouts Kam, as Raid force-marches him down the ramp.

"Not a problem," says Emie under her breath. Catching Calla's eye, she lifts her chin. She strides to the edge of the ramp, her back straight as a pine sapling. "Not a problem!" she yells after Kam.

I hurry forward to stand at Emie's side. "Good riddance."

Raid shoves Kam through the back gates—to the amusement of several colonists working in the machine yard.

"He's all right, that Raid," observes Dace as he steps up beside me. "I can see why you like him."

I glance over at Dace's pensive face. "Good friend."

Beside me, Emie snorts. "I'd like a friend like that," she says, elbowing me in the side.

You can have him soon. I bite the inside of my cheek to prevent myself from speaking aloud. Partially because, despite everything, I can't tell Emie my plans. Partially.

"That Kam kid is trouble." Calla circles around to face us. "You'd best be careful. He seems to be a few pulses short of a blast."

"You're the one who needs to be careful," says Dace. "Better keep your guard up, Calla."

"I always do," replies the cyber.

***

I leave Dace and Emie with Calla and make my way to the building that houses the colony's small lab. Although we don't conduct a lot of exploration or research, we still maintain a certain amount of scientific equipment.

I'm betting my mother's in the lab. She's been spending a lot of time there over the last few days conducting studies on the mineral Dace brought back from the cavern.

I push open the door and see I've guessed correctly. Mother's standing behind a tall table peering into a monitor built into its surface. She waves her hand over the screen and a three-dimensional model of Eco's terrain appears above the table. Whipping her fingers through the image, Mom zeroes in on a rock hill. She flicks the holographic model until the top layer disappears, leaving a dark image honeycombed with tunnels and caverns.

"Come in, Ann," she says, without taking her eyes off the model.

I close the door behind me and walk to the lab table. "That's what's underneath the surface?" I do my best to inject the proper amount of innocence into my tone.

Mom frowns. "We should have checked this out before, since we had the geological surveys from the initial satellite exploration of the planet. I mean, we knew about the underground water, and that caves existed, but apparently no one was interested in discovering much about them." She tenses her lips, creating two sharp lines that bracket her mouth. For a moment, she looks her age.

"Your parents tried." I pull a stool up to the table and sit across from her.

My mom slams her hand onto the model, collapsing the image into the monitor. "Yes, they did." Her hazel eyes examine me with detachment. "So, have you and the Keeling boy discovered anything else of interest?"

An image of the Selk arcing their bodies out of the water and diving back down, smooth as polished pebbles ... "No." I meet her gaze without blinking. "Well, we did find a cavern containing a small lake. Seems to be connected to some underground waterways."

"Where you found the sample."

"Yes. But Mom," I clutch my twitching hands in my lap, hiding them below the tabletop, "I just wonder if maybe we should slow down on this mining thing. Grandmother has a point; we wouldn't want to leave the colony vulnerable. And it seems there's plenty of time. No one's touched the mineral deposits in all these years—why rush now? Not like it's going to disappear."

Slender fingers smooth her silken cap of hair. "You're not going to side with your grandparents on this, I hope." She drops her hand and taps the tabletop. "I'd have thought you'd be even more anxious than I am. Your ticket off Eco just waiting to be collected."

"Yes, but … " Stupid not to have planned what I would say to her. "If we could just compromise, we wouldn't have to worry about any opposition. Collect enough of the mineral … "

"Promissium."

My nose wrinkles despite my best efforts to maintain a neutral expression. "Yeah, that. Anyway, collect enough to fill a few crates and Captain Patel can jet the samples off to his contacts. Let him line up the investors, and they can bring in new equipment for the mining. No one's placed in danger and we still get our credits and get off Eco." I manufacture a bright smile.

My mother studies me for a moment. She places her hands flat upon the table and leans forward. "I'm not waiting here until Captain Patel returns. When he leaves, I go with him. Don't look so shocked; surely you guessed this already. It's been decided— I'll assist Connor in locating and securing the proper mining partners. I am, after all, a geologist by trade." Her lips curve upward. Dace's art discussion pops into my mind, bringing with it a memory of pictures of beautiful women. If a painter were to capture Mom's expression, it would include that enigmatic smile so many portraits wear. "I want you to come with me, Ann."

"What about the others? Are we going to abandon grandmother and grandfather?" I slip off the stool and kick it to the side. "What about Dad?"

Mom lifts a hand and swirls it through the air. Her silver bracelet rings like tiny bells. "Oh, your father." She strokes the line of her jaw with one finger. "Let me tell you a story that involves your father. Just so you understand a little better why I must leave."

"You and Dad got married too young. I know that story." I cross my arms over my chest.

"No, you don't." Mom sighs and walks around the table. "You don't know anything about it, my darling daughter. Nothing at all." She leans back against the table, her arm brushing my elbow.

I pull my arms tighter about my body. "If you've fallen out of love, you should tell him. It's only fair."

Mom reaches out to tuck a sprig of hair behind my ear. "Oh my dear, how can one fall out of love if one never fell into it in the first place?"

I flinch but don't look away. "You mean you never loved Dad at all? Not even in the beginning?"

"No, I'm afraid I never did." Mom grabs the discarded stool and places it a few feet from me. She sits, her back very straight and her legs crossed at the ankles. "I was only seventeen, just your age, when my parents died. A horrible, slow, tortuous death from injuries, thirst, and starvation. I saw that holodisc, you know."

"I know," I whisper.

Mom tips up her chin, gazing over my head, her eyes fixed on the opposite wall. "I needed someone to hold me, to block out those images, to rock me to sleep at night. And there was your father. Such a good boy. So gentle and understanding. Your grandparents were kind as well. They took me in. They cared for me."

She's lost in her memories—wandering in the past, in a place of darkness that still shadows her face. I stare at the toes of my boots. Scuffed and cracked—I need to work some oil into the leather.

"Your father loved me. I knew that. I thought it would be enough—him loving me. I didn't really feel anything, you understand. I just knew his arms kept me from flying apart and the pressure of his lips kept me from screaming … " She shakes her head and drops her gaze. "Sorry. Too much information, I suspect."

I'm chewing on my pinky nail. I pull my finger from my mouth and stare at my hand. "Why did you marry, then? I mean, you could've waited. Until you were older. Until you felt better."

Mom smiles gently. "Well, then there was you, Ann."

My fingers curl into my palm. "You were pregnant? But you had a bioplant, so how … ?"

"I didn't have one. We didn't all have them implanted young, back then. My parents didn't think it was necessary. And it wasn't … before." She fingers her bracelet. "To be fair, when your grandparents realized, they didn't pressure me. Said they'd help raise you regardless. I think they knew we were too young. Or maybe they realized I wasn't in love with Jason—that I wasn't capable of love. Not then."

"But you married him anyway."

"I did. You know why?" She cocks her head to the side and stares at me with bright eyes, alert as some small, golden bird. "Because he promised he would get me off of Eco, that's why."

"He said that?" My nails cut into my skin. My father never talks about leaving Eco. When Mom or I express our desire to flee the planet by any means necessary, Dad calmly lists all the reasons why our dream is impossible.

"Yes, over and over. I hated Eco you know. I'd always despised it—the dust, the lack of opportunity, the tiny, ugly compound… I thought I'd go insane, surrounded by people with no more ambition than a boulder. I was trapped, with no chance for any change, stuck seeing the same faces, day after day. And after my parents died—after this godforsaken ball of stone swallowed them whole—my hatred grew faster than your grandmother's hydroponic vines." She leans back, swaying slightly on the stool. "Jason said if I married him, he'd make it his life's goal to get us both off this planet. He swore he'd do anything—steal credits if necessary—to book us passage with the first available trade ship. And I believed him."

"He didn't try?"

"You're getting ahead of the story." Mom crosses her hands, one over the other, in her lap. She looks like she's reciting a lesson for a holo class. "The first red flag appeared the day we married. I asked him about his plan, and he told me not to worry, he had it all figured out. But, just to be safe, we should wait until the baby came. So I waited. I ate right and did all the proper things to make sure you'd be healthy, and I waited."

"Seems like it would've been easier to leave, just the two of you, even with you pregnant, than dragging along an infant … " I say, then snap my mouth shut. Stupid, so stupid. The look on my mother's face confirms this assessment.

"Of course it would, and if I'd been in my right mind, I would've seen that excuse for what it was—a lie." Mom runs her hands up and down her bare arms, as if stricken by a chill. "Then, on the night you were born, when I was first cradling you in my arms, he told me that he'd miscalculated. You were so tiny, so fragile—we should wait until you were just a bit older. But he vowed, once again, that he would get all three of us off Eco. He'd take us to Earth, and we'd be one little, happy family."

I don't want to hear any more of this. "Not sure I understand what this has to do with your leaving with another man or fortune hunters mining some mineral on Eco."

"That night," continues my mother, as if I hadn't spoken, "holding you, my daughter, our child, I still believed him. I decided to wait, as long as necessary, for your father to fulfill his vow." She turns the full force of her beautiful hazel eyes on me. "Do you know why I named the mineral Promissium? A name I know is foolish. A name that makes you and others laugh. I did it to send a message. Because it is the one thing that will finally give me what I was promised, Ann."

She leaps to her feet, ignoring the clatter of the stool crashing to the floor behind her. In two strides she stands before me, and the fact that I am taller by several inches means nothing at all.

Before I can step back she locks her fingers around my forearms. "You ask me why I don't love your father? I'll tell you. It's not anything he did. It's what he didn't do."

I don't hear my mom's voice—not the voice of an adult, a leader of the Council, a fiercely independent, brilliant woman. I hear the voice of an angry child.

"He promised me." She gives me a shake. "He promised."

"I understand," I say, although I'm not sure this is true.

Her grip loosens. She slides her fingers down my arms, catching my fingers in a gentle clasp. "The point is," her honeyed tone returns, "I want you to come with me, Ann. This entire enterprise—it's for you."

I stare into her lovely eyes. It's quite possible she's telling the truth. Or, at least, believes she is. "You really want me to travel with you and Captain Patel?"

"I do. You see, I made you a promise when you were born, and unlike others, I always keep my promises. I swore I would give you what I could never have—our Earth heritage and a universe of opportunities."

I wiggle my fingers to make her drop my hands. "Your life isn't over. You still have time for yourself. For your own dreams."

"I'm doing this for you." Mom crosses to the far wall, to one of the lab's small, dust-coated windows. "Because I love you, Ann, despite what you may think. I've always loved you, ever since I first felt your heartbeat under my hand. You were so small—I had to protect you." She turns from the window to stare at me. "And that meant making sure you grew up independent and smart and strong enough to survive without me. Because I couldn't be sure I'd always be here. I couldn't promise this dreadful planet would allow us that luxury."

Our gazes lock. I swallow hard and rub at the indentations my nails bit into my palms. *I've always loved you.* She spoke those words. I think I believe her. But sometimes, the realization hits me, love might not be enough.

"I can't answer you now," I say, fighting the tremor in my voice. "I need time to think."

"That's fine." Mom walks toward me, her steps carefully measured. "Though Connor plans to leave as soon as we gather enough Promissium. That's why I want to go ahead and use some mining equipment, you see. It will take far too long if we try to gather the mineral by hand." Reaching me, she lays a cool hand against my cheek. "You don't want to wait that long to leave, do you?"

"I haven't said I was going." I don't know why I'm not jumping at this offer. It's everything I've always wanted.

Well, not exactly. I want my family, my entire family, to flee Eco with me. When I daydream I don't imagine leaving without my father or grandparents. I picture us living together on Earth. All of us.

As I study my mother's icy smile images flicker through my mind—Dace, radiating happiness during our recent swim and Raid, grinning with delight in the presence of the Selk. That's what I want for me and for my family. That joy.

Mom gives my cheek a gentle pat. "You think about it, Ann. Think long and hard." One more pat, this time on my shoulder, before she walks past me and out the door.

I don't turn to watch her leave. As the door clicks behind her, I observe dust motes sailing in the sunlight filtering through the windows. The tiny specks dance, sparkling like light reflected off water.

I've been handed my ticket, and by the one person I'd never dreamed would fulfill my dreams. It's strange how all I want to do is sink to the floor and weep.

CHAPTER SIXTEEN

I stumble out of the lab and make my way to the living quarters, keeping my head down. There's no one I want to see, and no one I want to see me. Not right now. No one but Emie.

Walking into her family quarters, I spy her mother standing at the microstove, swirling a large spoon around in a metal pot. I scratch at my nose, hiding my face behind my hand, and mutter something about meeting Emie.

"She's not back yet," says Ms. Winston. "Anything I can do, Ann?"

I duck my head. "No, no. Okay if I wait in her room?"

"Sure." Concern laces her voice. "We're having veggie stew tonight, if you want to stay for dinner."

I wave my hand in her direction and dash into Emie's bedroom.

I flop onto her bed and bury my face in her thin blanket, the tears flowing. I've always known my mom and dad didn't have a perfect marriage, but the idea that it was brought about by some weird combination of need and necessity—blended with a measure of unrequited love on my father's part—sends my mind reeling. It's as if the solid ground of Eco is falling away, hurling me into a cavern, and dashing me onto the rocks below.

After a time, my tears dry up. I roll over, my arms crossed behind my head. Above me, the edges of old pictures flutter. I sniff loudly and stare at the makeshift collage that covers the ceiling, remembering when Emie and I balanced on a crate piled on a chair to affix those pictures. It's comprised of laser photos of Andron Karl and his band, the StarKickers. At the time, Emie'd been obsessed with the doll-faced Andron for over two years, despite my insistence that the singer was merely the front for a computer-generated voice. Now, abandoned by even Emie, Andron's overly smooth face smiles indulgently down at me. "You thought I was a fake?" his rouged lips appear to say. "What about your life, Anna-Maria Solano? What about your family and all those memories stuffed in your head? Anything real about that?"

I toss one of Emie's pillows at the ceiling just as she enters the room.

"Using poor Andron for target practice again I see." Emie examines my face for a moment then sits next to me on the bed. "You've been crying."

"Brilliant deduction, Watson." My lips twitch. Emie and I used to read Arthur Conan Doyle stories aloud, challenging each other to solve the crimes before we reached the final paragraphs.

"Well, Sherlock, explicate the facts." Emie smiles and rubs my arm. "Something happen with Raid? Or … " Her dark eyebrows arch above her eyes. "Dace, maybe?"

I sit up, wrapping my arms about my knees. "No, nothing to do with boys. And anyway, you're the one with the bigger problem in that area."

"Not anymore." Emie whips out the ribbon threaded through her curls and tosses it to the floor.

"So Kam's out of the picture?"

"Poof." Emie spreads wide her hands. "Gone. Winked out like the stars on a cloudy night."

"He may not agree."

"Tough shit for him." The look Emie turns on me is startling in its certainty. "I trust Raid and the others to keep him in line, and my parents have been informed Kameron Frye's no longer a welcome guest. I hope you'll pass the word to your family as well."

"Of course." I clutch my knees closer to my chest and rock slowly. "It's my mom, Emie. She's leaving Eco with Connor Patel."

Emie's dark eyes widen. "Oh. Well … that sucks."

"You don't seem surprised."

"I've seen them, I mean … " Emie bites her lower lip.

"No, it's okay. Not exactly like they were subtle." I glance up at Andron's mocking mouth. "The thing is, Mom's asked me to come with her."

"When they leave Eco? Wow, Ann, it's what you always wanted."

It is. As everyone on Eco knows, it's my one and only dream. But somehow, after my recent experiences, the thought doesn't entice me. "We'd be leaving Dad and my grandparents behind."

"I assumed." Emie rolls over, balancing herself on one elbow, her chin pressed against the back of her hand. "You'd be leaving me too, of course. And Raid. But I've kind of expected it for a while. Doubt he has, though."

"He'll get over it." I tap her nose with one finger. "You can comfort him."

Emie snorts and bats my hand away. "We're not interchangeable."

"No, you're a much better person." I flop back onto the bed. "I don't know, Emie. Not certain it's what I want. Not like this, anyway."

"Well, I can tell you one thing—I know what I want."

I turn my head and examine her profile. A certain set to her jaw tells me she's deadly serious. "What's that?"

"I'm going to help the cybers fight for their rights." Emie tosses her dark curls. "No more of this stupid bigotry. They are people just like us, and they deserve to be treated as such."

"Going to lead the revolution?"

"If necessary." Emie sits up, pressing her back to the room's metal wall. "You could help me. Create an interactive campaign and upload it to the 'sphere. Blast out a petition on the holofone network ... "

"Using your hacking skills?"

Emie casts me an abashed grin. "Hmmm ... might have to do a major upgrade on those. But with time, I'll improve."

"I don't doubt it. But Emie, two girls on some half-assed planet aren't going to have much influence over the people who matter."

"Well," Emie holds out her hand, and when I grasp it, she pulls me into a sitting position, "that's where maybe it'd be good if you took your mom's offer. You could be my accomplice on Earth."

"Seriously?" I study her determined face for a moment. "Not sure I'll be in any position to help. At least, not right away."

"Your mom and the captain will be mixing with some big-money types, if what they say about Promissium is true. You could suck-up to them … "

I can't contain a gurgle of laughter. "This is me we're discussing, right?"

"Just give it some thought," says Emie without an answering smile. "I am going to accomplish this, Ann. Even if it takes me years and years. I've found the thing I was born to do, and I'm going to do it." She tugs on one of her curls. "And cut my hair. I believe I'll cut my hair short and stop working that cream into it. Let it go natural. Why should I care if some guy likes it better another way? This is me, and I think I'm pretty awesome all on my own."

"You've always been awesome." I lean in to give Emie a quick hug.

As my hands slide back she locks her arms about me and holds me tight. "You're awesome too, and don't you ever doubt it." She pushes me back, still holding onto my shoulders. "You just need to figure out what you really want. You—not your mom or Raid or anyone else. Just you."

"Yes." I meet her penetrating gaze without hesitation. "I think maybe I do."

***

Leaving Emie's room, I fend off her mom's attempt to convince me to stay for dinner and hurry to my family quarters.

I'm betting Mom hasn't come home yet, and quickly see I'm right. Ignoring the thought of where she might be, I notice Dad's slumped on the small cushioned bench that serves as our sofa, staring blankly into the screen of his holotablet.

"You all alone?" I stroll over and sit beside him.

He gives me a smile. "Not anymore."

His tablet is turned off. I tap the screen. "Just contemplating the infinite?"

"Something like that." He lays the tablet on the metal crate that functions as an end table. "You have that need-to-talk look. Something on your mind?"

I scoot closer and thread my arm through the crook created by his bent elbow. "Yes, but maybe I shouldn't bring it up."

He grins and pulls my arm tight against his. "Perfect way to ensure I'll make you. Good going, chica."

I take a deep breath. "The thing is, Mom said some stuff to me today. Shook me up."

Dad's grin fades. "Let me guess." He stares at the opposite

wall. "She told you we had to get married and that I've failed her miserably ever since?"

"Not quite in those words." I chew on the inside of my cheek a moment before continuing. "She did say you promised to take us off Eco. Apparently, several times."

Dad's gusty sigh fills the silence. "She's right about that." He slides his arm away from mine. "Ah well, since she's opened the forbidden box, I might as well let you see all the demons inside." He sits up straighter. "I actually made a vow—twice. Once when I proposed and again on the night you were born."

So Mom hadn't been lying, or even embellishing the truth. I squirm on the lumpy padding covering the bench.

"The thing is, I meant it. I truly did. Although … " Dad's averts his face. "I admit it was mainly because I wanted your mom to say 'yes' the first time."

"Because you loved her?"

"Actually, I'd say adored her. It's a little different." Dad shoots me a rueful smile. "I love you, and your grandparents. Your mother— that was something else. Not so healthy, maybe." He leans back, crossing his arms behind his head to act as a buffer against the cold metal of the wall. "There weren't as many kids in the beginning, of course. Not that we have a lot now, but back then … just a handful in any one age group. But even if there'd been thousands, Tara would've stood out. You must understand—I knew your mom all my life. She was always there—a brilliant blond angel. So beautiful, even as a child. I used to follow her around and try to give her things. Bright pebbles, a rare piece of candy, anything like that. Until her parents got worried and told me to back off.

Actually, they told my parents to tell me."

"Bet that went over well." I catch his fleeting smile.

"Mama fumed but warned me to keep my distance. Still, there was little chance that Tara and I wouldn't be thrown together over the years. But I hung back, just made polite conversation, or simply smiled. Worshipped from afar."

There's an edge of anger in his tone that surprises me. I pat his knee. "Until her parents died."

"Yes. They were going to leave Eco, you know. I was going to lose her. Forever." Dad stares at the ceiling, his expression blank. "Her parents were taking her to Earth. They'd worked overtime, saving credits from geologic consulting work on the 'sphere. The final exploration of the rock hills was part of that. One last job and they'd have enough for their passage. They'd made arrangements with a trader scheduled to land on Eco in a few weeks." His lips twitch into an ironic smile. "Tara was already packed."

"I didn't know that." I tap the toe of my boot against the floor. Mom has never mentioned this detail.

"Of course, that all changed when her parents died. The promised credits evaporated when your grandparents passed away without a will. That holodisc surfaced. And your mom fell apart. I always wondered how much of it was about losing them and how much was ... "

"Losing her chance for a life on Earth?"

Dad glances over at me. "A blend of the two, I suspect. Loss and frustration and anger—it wrecked her. She started doing crazy stuff. Drinking that swill Doug Frye cooks up, racing her bike like she was pursued by demons ... I don't know, maybe she was. At any rate, everyone tried to help. Even the kids her age—we did what we could. The funny thing is, my presence calmed her. She seemed better when she was with me. I listened, I held her, I never judged … " Dad drops his arms and turns to me, taking my hands in his. "I adored her. As always. Constant as the Angel Star."

"You saved her."

Dad tightens his grip on my fingers. "No. I helped her pull herself back together. But I wasn't doing it just for her. I know that now. After all these years, I can confess the truth. I took advantage of her, Ann. I used her need for comfort because I wanted—I needed—her. So desperately." He shakes his head. "I shouldn't tell you this, you shouldn't have to hear it. But I know your mother is leaving Eco. She's found someone else to fulfill my vow. And even though I'm angry, and hurt, and just want to break things, I can't allow you to think the worst of her. She doesn't deserve that, no matter what."

"You know?" I can only manage a ragged whisper.

"Yes. I'm not quite as blind as many think." He lifts our clasped fingers and presses his stubbly cheek against the back of my hand. "Don't hate her, Ann. That will only hurt you in the end. And I never want anything to hurt you."

I lean into him, resting my head on his shoulder. "I'm sorry, Papa. I know you still love her."

"Oh, chica." Dad's grip on my fingers loosens. He drops my hands and pushes me back. Tears well in his eyes as he gazes into my face. "I wish that were true. But I've been worn away, like those pebbles you used to bring me when you were a little girl.

Remember the one with the hole in it? So perfect, you thought some creature or alien being must have created it?"

I nod as I wipe my eyes with my fingers.

"Remember what I told you? That it was simply the wind blowing sand particles, polishing away layers of the stone?"

I do remember. A day where I sat in his lap and my mother ... my mother was nestled close to us, examining my special stone. "You said it just kept being eaten away, in microscopic bites, by the sand. Until one day a tiny fissure appeared, and the fissure opened into a crack and the crack spread into a hole."

Dad's eyes are closed, and I wonder if he's reliving that moment as well. "Not blasted away, not cut away, just worn away ... by what, chica?"

"Time."

My father leans in and kisses me on the forehead. "Yes, by time." He stands and holds out his hands. "You understand what I'm saying?"

"Yes." I allow him to pull me to my feet. "But sometimes, love grows stronger over time, doesn't it Papa? I mean, I hope it does. I want to believe it can."

"It can." A smile illuminates his face. "All you have to do is look at your grandparents." He swings my hands like he used to do when I was small enough for him to lift me off the floor. "And I love you more today, mi hija, than on the day you were born, though I would've sworn that was impossible."

A fine web of lines radiates from the corners of his deep brown eyes. I realize he's no longer young. Time, wearing everything away. "She's asked me to come with her."

"I see." His smile fades. "And will you?"

"I don't know yet."

"Okay, that's fair." He studies me for a moment. "You have to do what's best for you, Anna-Maria. Not for me or for her—for you."

"Funny, Emie just told me that."

"She's a smart girl." Dad lifts one hand to touch my cheek. "So are you. I'll be proud of you whatever you decide. Never forget that."

I cover his hand with mine. "I never forget anything you tell me." My fingers fall away slowly. As I head for my bedroom I call back over my shoulder, "And time won't ever change that."

CHAPTER SEVENTEEN

"**H**ot in here." Dace wipes the sweat from his forehead with the edge of his sleeve.

"Duh, it's a greenhouse." I tap one of the black nutrient bins with the toe of my boot. "Want to help me move this, or are you happy playing boss?"

"Sure." Dace squats down to get a good grip on the bin. "Just you and your grandmother take care of all this?"

"No." I grunt and tighten my stomach muscles as we lift the heavy container. "Over there across the aisle is fine." After we set down the bin, I wipe my hands on my already stained jeans. "Several people are trained to work in the greenhouse. It's too important to rely on just one or two colonists. But grandmother runs the place, and she and I spend the most time working here."

Dace straightens and casts a glance over the jungle of vines and other hanging vegetation. "You'd starve without it."

"Yes." I've known this fact all my life, but hearing it from someone else makes it feel real. The work we do, my grandmother and I, is important. Perhaps not all that exciting or challenging, but essential. I look about me at the flourishing plants, vines, and dwarf trees. Our colony couldn't survive without these fruits and vegetables. Simple as that. Yet—I glance over at my grandmother—not easy. It's taken the lifelong devotion of someone who doesn't really get much credit.

Dace has been shadowing me all morning. He claims he needs to understand the colony's infrastructure for his research. Pushing back the damp hair that clings to his forehead, he casts another glance about the greenhouse. "Something to be proud of—keeping all this going." His gaze lands on my grandmother, who's testing the level of phosphorous in one of the nutrient solutions.

She gives Dace a smile and peers into her portable monitor. "It's taken some doing, I can tell you that."

"The entire colony would have failed if Grandmother hadn't spent night after night here in the early days, coaxing the plants to grow. Or so Grandfather tells me. Of course, you could say 'force' instead of 'coax.'"

Grandmother shakes her finger at me. "Always with the smart mouth, nieta." She pockets her monitor and meets Dace's speculative stare. "It wasn't that difficult. Easier than raising children." Her eyes focus on me. "Or grandchildren."

Dace turns his head but can't quite hide his grin. I study his profile for a moment, wondering where he acquired his confidence. I know from our conversations he was raised in near-poverty and tormented by his peers over his lack of a father. Yet despite his outward diffidence, he's not intimidated by others— no matter how old or wise or powerful. I guess it's his devotion to research that trumps his fears. His dreams of discovery must outweigh any sense of inadequacy.

It'd be nice to have a dream like that—to study something that fascinates you, that you can pursue with interest your whole life. I shake my head. Stupid thoughts. I have a dream too. So what if it's just leaving one place for another?

A sharp clang rings through the moist air. The front door vibrates as if the metal has been struck by a hammer.

I jog to the door and open it a crack. A slice of Kam's pale face greets me.

"Open up," he says, his visible eye narrowed to a green slit.

"Who's there?" Grandmother's voice sails over the sound of the air-circulation system.

I open the door wider. "Kameron Frye and his dad and uncle and a few others."

A small knot of people stand in the narrow path that runs between the greenhouse and the domed animal pens. Standing just behind Kam is my mother, with Captain Patel at her side.

Dace is right behind me. "Looking for someone in particular?"

"Not someone," replies Kam, stepping back as he slaps a thin metal pipe against his calloused palm.

My grandmother strolls over, pausing to slide a stun gun off a shelf near the door. She studies Dace and me for a minute while arming the gun. "Your mother's outside."

I swallow hard and nod.

"They want two of my fans for their mining machine. Need cooling elements, they say. Well, I say we need food more."

"Will two fans make that much difference?" asks Dace. His expression is entirely serious.

"Perhaps not," says my grandmother, "but where does it end? We don't have that many spare parts lying around. I give them the equipment today, and then some of my fans go on the blink tomorrow. What then, Dacian Keeling?"

"Dace." Those dark eyes survey my grandmother with interest. "Good point. Truthfully," he shuffles his feet on the rough grate of boards covering the concrete floor, "I totally agree with you, Ms. Solano. Or is it Dr. Solano?"

"Ms. will do." My grandmother's gaze brims with approval. "Dace."

My fingernails bite into my palms again. "We need to do something."

Grandmother puts out a hand to halt my progress toward the open door. "You're not going out there, Anna-Maria."

I flip my braid back over my taut shoulder. "Mom might listen to me."

"Maybe." Grandmother tightens her grip on my arm. "But I'm not willing to take that chance. Besides, your mother isn't the only one out there, and even she can't control every loose cannon on Eco." She turns toward the entrance. "I'm going to have a little chat with our visitors. You two stay behind me—understand?"

Her eyes bore into me. I nod. "Bien."

Leveling the stun gun, she braces one foot against the doorjamb.

Dace leans into me, peering over my shoulder. "Kam looks like he's itching for a fight."

"He always looks like that." I spy Raid stepping out of the shadows between the dairy and the rec hall, Emie at his side. The two of them remain several yards away from Mom's group. "Shhh... Grandmother's talking."

"I told you 'no' before—guess you didn't listen. Now, stand down."

My mother's words ring out amid the hum of voices. "Paloma, don't be difficult. We simply want to borrow a few things."

"Not happening."

"This is foolishness." Mom steps forward, separating herself from the others. "You're not stupid—you must understand what this opportunity means. Once we've gathered enough Promissium to guarantee a contract with a mining company, we can all leave Eco. Let the miners work while we reap the profits. We don't need to concern ourselves with long-term survival."

Out of the corner of my eye, I see my father and grandfather appear around the edge of one of the domes. They are jogging, their eyes fixed on the greenhouse.

"You're assuming we all want to leave, Tara." The business end of the stun gun never twitches. It's pointed directly at my mother's forehead.

"And why wouldn't you?" Mom stands as still as a sentinel. "What is there on this godforsaken planet for you? For anyone?"

"Our life is here."

Dad strides forward and lays a hand on Mom's arm. "Enough, Tara."

"What kind of life is that?" asks Mom, without acknowledging my father's touch.

With Dad's body blocking her aim, my grandmother lowers her gun. "The only life you've ever known. The life you should be protecting—for your child, if no one else."

Dace grips my shoulder. I must've made some sound.

"I'm going to give my daughter more than that." Light glints off Mom's gilt hair. "I'm giving her the universe."

"Not with my fans, you're not. Besides, Anna-Maria is in here with me." Grandmother leans to one side so the crowd can catch a good glimpse of Dace and me. "Along with the actual discoverer of your precious mineral. Perhaps he should have more of a say in what happens next."

Someone shouts something about spacers as Connor Patel moves closer to Mom's side. "Dacian, enough of this nonsense. Come out of the building. No sense mixing in a colony dispute."

"It's more than that." Dace pushes past me. Grandmother makes a grab for his arm but he's too quick for her. "This whole thing's moving too fast, Uncle Connor."

Dace faces off with his uncle. One of the Frye brothers yells out, "Just give us the damn fans," but grandmother simply motions for me to join her just outside the doorway as my father and grandfather take up positions flanking Dace.

"Jason, Jason, Jason," Mom murmurs. Toe-to-toe with my dad, she stares up into his stoic face. "As always, standing in my way."

Kam bounds out of the group, flexing his hands. "I say we just shove 'em aside and take what we need."

My mother waves him back. "Not yet."

I'm astonished when Kam stops in his tracks, but a quick glance at his face tells the story. Of course he's fallen under my mother's spell. It wouldn't have been that hard to win Kam over. She probably graced him with one of her enchanting smiles and talked to him as if he were a grown man. I make a disgusted noise. Grandmother glances over at me, pursing her lips.

Mom looks my father up and down. "I still think reason may prevail."

"Since you've abandoned reason, not sure how that will work." Dad keeps his gaze focused over Mom's head.

Grandfather scans the crowd. "I see you back there, Efrain Medina. So who's working on that broken pump you swore to fix today? And Lyssa Lee, finished with that fabrication project yet? No? Didn't think so. Bunch of troublemakers. Go back to work, the lot of you, and leave my wife alone."

"We are working!" Even Mom can't prevent Kam from diving into the middle of a fight. He stalks toward my grandfather, who holds up one hand to halt his approach. "We're the ones trying to excavate spacer boy's mineral goldmine. Then we can all collect credits and blast off this rock. That *work* enough for you, old man?" Gaining courage from the noises of approval, he takes another step and fires off a rude gesture.

"Watch yourself, Kameron Frye." My grandmother's fingers tighten around the grip of her stun gun.

"Or what?" Kam drops the pipe and stands, legs spread apart, fists clenched at his sides. "You gonna blast me? Nah, I don't think so."

"This is unproductive." My mother turns to the captain. "Connor, can you talk some sense into your nephew? My family's apparently past all hope." She stares directly at me.

I meet her gaze without flinching. "There's actually a plan that might please everyone, if you'd listen. Dace thought of it."

"Oh, so the spacer's making the rules now?" Kam sneers at me before turning to address the milling crowd. More colonists have arrived, obviously drawn by the commotion. Most seem content to hang out at the fringes, casting a wary eye on the proceedings. "That what we want? Strangers landing here, mucking about on our planet, telling us how to do things?"

Shouts erupt and several colonists push their way forward. Most take up positions behind Kam. But two people walk past him to join my father and grandfather in flanking Dace. One is Emie.

The other is Raid. "Back down, Kam."

"Protecting your honey, are you?" Kam insolently shoves his hands in his pockets. "Even though she's probably banging junior scientist over there?"

Raid's attempt to lunge at Kam is curtailed by Grandfather gripping his shoulder and yanking him back.

"No need to fight, son," says Grandfather, releasing Raid. "Don't soil your hands."

Mom's eyes narrow as she examines Kam. Sure, she's happy to make use of him, but I know she won't permit anyone to insult me. Her pride's too great, if nothing else. Kam doesn't realize it, but he's just made a dangerous enemy.

"Enough of this." Mom turns back to my grandmother. "Very

well, Paloma. We won't pursue this matter any further today. But we will have our machines, all the same."

"I'm sure." A triumphant smile lights Grandmother's face. "But you won't have my fans."

Mom's gaze flits from Grandmother to the others opposing her, coming to rest on Dad. "We'll find another way. The mining will proceed, with or without your blessing."

As Mom walks away, Dace chases her and clutches her arm. "You can't rush this! You don't know what's at stake!"

She turns and stares at him, shaking off his hand. Disdain emanates from her like a scent. "Whatever do you mean? I know exactly what I'm doing, as does your uncle."

Dace's lower lip quivers. "No, you don't. None of you does. You don't understand what you'll be destroying … "

"Dace!" I dart forward, inserting my body between him and my mother. "Don't say another word."

"I must."

"You promised." I take hold of his hands and stare beseechingly into his face.

Dace shakes his head. "I'm sorry, Ann." He pulls his hands from my grip and steps back to address the growing crowd. "The truth has to be told. You need all the facts before you make this decision."

"What do you mean?" Captain Patel glances from Dace to my mother.

"It's no one's fault. Or maybe it's mine." Dace lifts his chin. "I should've said something sooner. But I promised Ann … "

"Ann?" Emie's lips tremble as she turns to me.

All our talks, and I've still been keeping secrets. Yes, I know, Emie. I know I've failed you. I stiffen my spine and keep my focus on Dace. "You can't do this. We had a deal."

"Some things are more important." Dace's gaze locks with mine. There's trace of pity in his look, which only infuriates me more.

Behind him, Raid's expression shifts from astonishment to confusion. I narrow my eyes at Dace. "More important than promises?"

"Than promises that should never have been made, yes."

Connor Patel ignores my mother's fierce glare. With his attention on his nephew, Connor absently rubs the back of his neck with one hand. "I'm confused. What's this all about, Dacian?"

"You promised!" I hate that this comes out as a wail, that my entire body is vibrating with anger.

"You aren't alone on this planet," says the boy who kissed me in the lake.

"Damn you." I spit out the words.

"How so?" My mother moves closer.

Dace shoots me an apologetic look and plunges ahead. "There's another life form living here. Not just insects and lizards, but a species of mammal that seems to possess a high level of intelligence. They live underground—in the lakes and rivers that flow through the caverns beneath our feet. Ann and I discovered them. Or they discovered us—I'm not quite sure which."

"You never said." Emie's eyes, focused on me, brim with tears.

"I had my reasons." I lift my head to meet the disapproving gazes of my family. Not just my mother, but my grandmother, father, and grandfather are staring at me with disappointment. The muscles in my fingers twitch. I want to hit someone. Preferably Dace.

"Why did you keep this a secret, son?" asks my grandfather.

"Because Ann asked me to. Because ... " Dace's eyes say "sorry" even as he forges ahead, shredding my dreams. "Because there's more to it than just a new species. Ann can understand them, you see, at least on a basic level. Some type of mental communication. Not me—I hear chirps and tweets and barks. Ann hears words."

Mom clasps her hands in front of her, clenching and unclenching her fingers. "Now you're talking nonsense. Communication? I might buy the existence of some unknown species, but I doubt my daughter can talk to them."

Dace stands his ground, apparently unmoved by the rumble of discordant voices rising from the crowd. "It's true. Ann can tell you."

I tighten my lips and stare at my boot tips.

Dace sighs and turns back to the others. "I did an analysis, and discovered ... " his voice is laced with awe, " ... a miracle."

"Bullshit," says Kam.

I look up to catch Kam snatching up the pipe he'd dropped at his feet earlier. "So, maybe you found some creatures you want to protect or something. You've got that Greener stench about you, so I'm not surprised. But I ain't buying any miracle crap."

"Please continue," says Mom, flicking her hand toward Kam as if to toss aside his interruption. "What is this so-called miracle, Dacian?"

She's following Connor Patel's habit of using his full name. I glance over at my father. He displays no emotion, just some rapid blinking.

Dace takes a deep breath and surveys the colonists gathered before him. "Ann can understand their communications because she shares a snippet of DNA with these creatures. I suspect it may be true for everyone born and raised on Eco."

The sharp bleat of a goat is the first sound to shatter the silence that falls after this revelation.

"That's … " Kam seems to be straining to think of some comment worthy of the fear and disgust painted across his face. "Crap. Utter crap. We're one-hundred-percenters, spacer. Not some sorry mutants."

Dace's nose twitches, sniffing back a snort of disgust. "For your information, I'm not a spacer. I was born and raised on Earth. But that's not relevant. The important thing is—you're tied to these creatures by more than simple proximity. I think that's worth further research before you charge in and destroy their habitat."

My grandmother moves out of the doorway to join Grandfather and Dad. "You have proof of this DNA mutation, Dace?"

"Yes. Ann can confirm it." He looks at me.

Everyone looks at me. I'm drowning in a sea of eyes, all focused on my face. Expectant. Nervous. Angry. Terrified. I stare at a point above their heads. A thin wisp of cloud, curled like the tail of the Selk … "Don't look at me," I mutter.

"I can confirm it."

I throw up my head to meet Raid's tortured gaze. "Not you too," I mouth silently, not trusting my voice.

Raid takes up a position beside Dace. "I've seen these creatures, and I heard what they said, just like Ann. Not words, exactly, but thoughts. Communication, whatever you want to call it." His eyes seek me out. "Sorry, Ann, but I agree with Dace. We can't allow decisions to be made when people don't know the whole truth."

I stare into two pairs of dark eyes, both beautiful. Examine two mouths, both of which I've kissed. Consider two separate, very different, boys, both of whom have betrayed me.

"You're saying we all carry this mutation?" Mom glowers as Connor Patel moves a few steps from her side.

"Not sure, but I suspect … "

The crowd erupts in a frenzy of movement and sound. I survey the scene as if standing outside one of our domes, looking in. Arms waving, voices barking questions, my grandfather pulling Grandmother away from one of the screaming Frye brothers, Kam lunging for Dace and Raid intervening, punching Kam in the jaw.

"I can't … " I don't even realize I've spoken aloud until Emie turns to me with a question in her eyes. "This. I can't do this."

Emie reaches for me, but I shove her hand away. Stumbling, I run from the greenhouse, praying no one follows me.

They don't. I am alone. I stand at the back door of the living quarters, my hand on the latch. The noise from the greenhouse pulses in my ears. I cast one final glance at the milling crowd before I whip open the door and dart inside.

There's a rhythmic refrain pounding against the bones of my skull—must go, can't stay, must escape.

I reach my bedroom without remembering how I got there. I grab my emergency pack and toss in some extra clothes and supplies. I'll make a stop at the storehouse on my way out to scoop up some extra food and water.

Can't stay.

Must escape.

CHAPTER EIGHTEEN

My bike roars through the silent wasteland of Eco. The rushing air sandblasts my face, drying the tears that well in my eyes and drip down my cheeks. My helmet, still hanging from a handlebar, bangs against one knee. I know I'm courting death, riding fast without protection. But it doesn't seem important right now.

Dace has betrayed me. Raid has betrayed me. The entire colony will discover our genetic anomaly. Earth's doors will be closed to me. My parents are separating. I've hurt Emie. Everything's been smashed into fragments.

I gun my engine. Already farther out than I've ever traveled, I keep my eyes focused on the horizon.

I ride with no regard for time. As I speed over the bleak landscape, my anger fades to a dull throb of frustration. Farther on, even that sensation drifts away, like shredded clouds. I feel nothing. I'm hollow as a stalk of bamboo.

Finally, the slowing of the bike forces me to stop. Climbing off, I pop up the solar collectors that hug the frame. A little time to recharge and I can be on my way. To where, I have no idea.

I'm pulled up beside a rock hill. This one is taller than those nearer the compound, its pinnacle piercing the clear sky like a dagger. I slide my bags off the bike and stumble over to the base of the rocks, seeking a little shade.

There's a faint scent of water. I glance around and notice a gap in the stones. If I move a few of the rocks aside I suspect I'll discover the entrance to another cavern. But what would be the point? I press my back against the rough edges of stones. It's okay to be uncomfortable—hot and sweaty and covered in a film of dirt and sand. It suits my mood.

After drinking some water, I rummage in the bags for a snack. My fingers close about an apple. I lift it out, balancing it in the center of my palm. An apple, grown on our fruit trees. Evidence of my grandmother's struggle, over so many years, to keep an abandoned colony alive. No one can say she hasn't done anything with her life.

I want that—the knowledge my life means something, that I'm doing something that matters, something important. I stare at the half-eaten apple, thinking of Emie's mission to help the cybers. Considering my mother's plans. I want something too. Something that benefits someone besides myself.

As I toss the apple core, I notice a few of the native lizards scurrying about my boots. One darts toward my empty hand, which is lying, palm up, on a rock. The creature touches my fingertip with its tiny snout.

I hold my hand perfectly still. Perhaps the lizard smells apple, or perhaps it's merely curious—at any rate, it leaps up. Clinging to my finger like a curling vine, the creature climbs forward.

Once it's safely settled in my palm, I lift my hand level with my eyes. The lizard's moss-green eyes blink, its snout twitches.

"Hello," I say. Held up to the light, its scales flash a spectrum of colors. "You're beautiful, you know."

The creature's tiny claws scrabble at my palm, pricking like pine needles.

"I won't hurt you." I know it can't understand me. I calm my twitching hand and fight to regulate my breathing. Slow everything down, until all I hear is the sifting of sand over rock and all I see is the small, living being before me.

The lizard curls until its snout touches its tail. Lowering filmy lids over its bright eyes, it rests quietly in my palm.

Unprotected. Unafraid.

I raise my eyes to look out over the surrounding area. More rock hills dot the horizon like abstract sculptures, their dark edges shimmering under the bright sun. The ground's draped in a glittering veil of golden sand, swirled with the pewter hues of dust. The sky is the color of a crocus petal—pale blue veined with periwinkle.

"You're beautiful too," I say.

The sound of a solar bike and a whirl of dirt drag my gaze away from contemplation of Eco's familiar yet somehow newly discovered landscape. I gently lower the lizard to the ground, using one fingernail to deposit it into the safety of a rock cleft.

The figure walking toward me is not the person I expect. "Hello, Calla," I say, and rise to my feet. "What're you doing out here?"

The cyber pulls off her helmet. "Tracking you, of course."

"Who gave you that job?" I slap the dust off my jeans and try not to stare at Calla's poreless face.

"My boss. Just following orders himself. He may still be the captain, but apparently your mom's now calling the shots." Calla runs her gloved fingers through her cropped hair. "She's pretty freakin' frantic over your disappearance, kid."

"I'm fine."

"I can see that." Calla strides closer, until we are standing face-to-face. "Decided to take a little walkabout, did you?"

"A what?"

"A journey into the wilderness. A spiritual quest. Something like that. I dunno, my mum used to mention it. Heard it from her parents."

"Maybe," I reply, thinking of the lizard and the way Eco now looks different to me. "So my mom sent you to retrieve me?"

"Something like that." Calla's gaze moves over my bags. "You have any water? Set off without."

"That was stupid."

"Yeah, well ... " Calla sits down in one smooth motion, crossing her legs up under her. "I've been known to do some stupid shit, kid. Now, you have water or what?"

I grab up the bags and settle beside her. Handing her one of my water flasks, I decide to ask the bold question. "That how you got hurt? Doing something stupid?"

Calla's expression doesn't change but her fingers tighten about the flask with frightening ferocity. "S'pose you could say that. I was stupid enough to try to save some dumbass's life." She takes a deep swig of the water. "Any other questions?"

I know that's my signal to shut up, but I don't owe this cyber anything. The way things are going, she won't be doing me any favors escorting me back to the compound. "Actually, yes."

Calla hands back the flask, her artificial eyes reflecting the light in a distinctly unnerving fashion. "Fire away, then. Not like I want to make the trip back on that piece of crap you call a bike anytime soon."

"How many surgeries did you have to have?"

"Too many." Calla tugs off one glove, exposing a gleaming metal hand. "S'posed to have gotten the hands covered in cyber-skin too, but that was just one procedure too many. Figured gloves were the way to go." She wiggles the mechanical fingers. "Freaky, right?"

I swallow hard. "I've seen weirder things."

Calla's lips twitch. "Huh. Anyway, it's a good trick to pull when some spacer gets too up close and personal, if you know what I mean."

I ignore the implications of that remark. "You ever see your family? I mean, since your accident?"

"Once. Met up on Moonbase One, so it wasn't that far for them to travel." Calla lowers her head so I can no longer see her eyes. "But now, with my sister so sick, it wouldn't work. She couldn't make even that short a trip. Guess she'll die without seeing me again in person. Holo visits will have to do."

"Emie mentioned that." I examine Calla's silky, somehow wrong hair. "They can't give you a pass for that? A twenty-four hour visit to Earth, just to see her? Not like you plan to stay."

Calla lifts her head and stares into my eyes. "No cybers allowed on Earth. Not for any reason, or any bit of time. That's the law. Well, except for the wealthy and powerful, of course."

"What do you mean?"

"Aw, come on, kid. You think somebody in one of the leading families gets in an accident—you know, skiing or skydiving or one of those other stupid things they do to pass the time—you think they don't get a cyber-upgrade if they lose some body part? Or if some glam babe gets burnt while undergoing one of those weird physical enhancement procedures—you think she's going to walk around with scars when cyber-skin's available?"

I tug on my braid. "But they don't allow anyone on Earth who's a cyber. They'd be deported."

Calla points one of her metal fingers at me. "*You'd* be deported. *I'd* be deported. But the ones that run things ... nah. Rules is rules, unless you're above the law."

"That isn't fair."

"Tell me about it." Calla slumps back against the rocks. "Your friend, Emie, she's been researching stuff. She didn't tell you this before?"

No, she didn't. Probably because she knew I wouldn't really listen. "Dace found a genetic anomaly in my DNA."

"Heard that." Calla shoots me a look that seems to hold a trace of compassion. "Something about sharing genes with those water creatures you found?"

"Yeah." I shift my weight, leaning closer to the cyber. "Means I'm not a one-hundred-percenter."

"That sucks."

"They won't let me in now, will they? On Earth, I mean."

"Nope."

Although Calla's expression can only change slightly, there's something in her eyes that tells me, clearer than words, what she's thinking.

We're the same, she and I. Those gates are barred to both of us.

Calla wheezes out a sigh and gazes out across the quiet landscape. "What was this place supposed to be, anyway? Good atmosphere, decent weather—was it meant to be sold off to some rich bastards?"

"I guess you could say that." A rock digs into the back of my head. I ignore it. "NewSkies—that was the corporation that owned the planet—planned to develop it bit by bit. Make copies—facsimiles, my mom calls them—of Earth's most beautiful landscapes. My grandparents were part of the first team sent out. They were supposed to terraform one section. Bring water up to the surface, fill in some of caverns below, put up a dome and all that. So there'd be this—model, I guess you could call it—for people to look at. Complete with lakes and streams and trees and grass."

"Hah." Calla's snort sounds like rusty gears. "Just like those ancient subdivisions they used to build on Earth."

"I guess." I frown, not remembering this from my holo history lessons.

"So who was going to buy these estates? I assume that's what they planned? Can't see rich Earthers zooming out here to snap up some resort property."

"Oh, it was meant for rich people, all right—spacers or others who didn't want to live on Earth."

"Or couldn't." Calla slides her glove back over her artificial hand.

"Or couldn't. Anyway, my grandparents weren't supposed to stay forever. They were poor—they had to sign up with NewSkies to get an education and any chance for advancement—but they were one-hundred-percenters. They only signed a ten-year contract. When their time was up, they'd collect a load of credits and return home, while another team arrived to take over."

"That was the plan, huh? But then NewSkies goes bust and just leaves them here, without enough equipment or supplies, and not a dome in sight. Well, except for those animal pens."

"We did get the planet." I wiggle my toes inside my boots. My feet feel like they're falling asleep. "NewSkies had to give the deed to the colonists, in equal shares. So at least we do own Eco."

"Little enough for all your trouble." Calla stares up into the sky. "So, the thing is, why didn't NewSkies let their first team in on the existence of these water creatures? The Selk, that's what the kid calls them, right?"

"Right." I scramble to my feet, grabbing one of the protruding rocks for balance. "They didn't know, I guess. My grandparents didn't have a clue. I don't think anyone did."

Calla stands without reaching for any support. "NewSkies would've. You know how much data those companies collect on the planets they own? I've seen some of that shit in the military. Hell, even in some of the deals the captain's brokered. There are reams of that stuff. Satellite imagery, thermal scans, bio scans, computer models ... You name it, they do it. So don't tell me NewSkies didn't know all about these Selk."

"They told them—my grandparents and the others—they told them to draw up the water and fill in those caverns ... "

"So you said."

"But if they knew, and wanted to do the terraforming anyway... " I twist the end of my braid around my hand. Of course, New Skies never told the terraformers. If the team knew, they might have refused to carry out the orders. NewSkies wouldn't have cared about some indigenous species. Just like they didn't care about the colonists they left stranded after the company went bankrupt. "It wouldn't have killed all the Selk, not in the beginning," I say, puzzling it out. "They could have moved to another location. But eventually ... " I clench my fingers tighter. "Once they developed the entire planet, or most of it, that would've been the end of the Selk."

"Sounds like it." Calla studies me dispassionately. "That thought bother you?"

An image of the water creatures, leaping and diving around me, fills my mind. My grandparents could have been instrumental in their destruction, long ago, without even knowing it.

Now there's another threat to the Selk's existence. And I know all about it.

"I'm ready to go back now."

"All right. Let's ride, kid."

"No racing," I say, remembering Dace.

"No promises," replies the cyber. Her lips ratchet up into that mechanical smile.

Funny. It doesn't seem to unnerve me anymore.

CHAPTER NINETEEN

It's quiet inside the gates of the compound. Calla and I park our bikes near the rec hall and approach Trent, who's perched on a crate beside the front doors.

"Where'd everyone go?" I ask.

Trent jerks his thumb toward the doors. "Inside, most of them. 'Cept for the Council—they called an emergency meeting."

So my mom will be busy with that. I wonder where Dad and my grandparents are. "What's going on in there?"

"I dunno." Trent's staring at Calla.

The cyber meets his fascinated gaze without blinking. "The rest of the colony's inside?"

"Well, not everyone." Trent drops his eyes and scratches at the scabs on his elbow. He's being trained on the wind turbines, just like Kam. Unlike Kam, he doesn't really have the athletic ability to do the work without incurring some injuries. "Some followed the Council to their meeting and several went back to work. The ones inside are arguing about Dace's theory and whether we should test everyone in the colony."

"You don't have an opinion?" asks Calla.

"Anybody likely to listen if I did?" Trent's blue eyes hold a glimmer of rage. He turns his focus on me. "So—sure as hell doesn't seem like I'll be attending a university on Earth, does it?"

"We don't know for sure if everyone carries the same mutation…"

"Yeah." Trent slumps back against the metal walls of the hall. "That's what they're arguing about. To test or not to test." He crosses his arms over his narrow chest and gazes moodily across the courtyard. "Doesn't matter. If we stay here, it won't make any difference. But if we aren't one-hundred-percenters and try to land on Earth, we'll be kicked back into space. So—who cares?"

"Better to know, so you don't have false hope." Sympathy laces Calla's strange voice.

Trent's disgruntled expression doesn't change. "I suppose."

One of the front doors bangs open and Lily dashes out. "You see Emie anywhere?" she asks Trent, before glancing over at Calla and me.

"Not recently," he replies.

"We just got here." I slap a spot of dust off my jeans. "Why? She missing or something?"

Lily shrugs. "She and Raid were in the rec hall with us, but they left by the back door. Said they were gonna go look for that spacer kid. Mom thinks they should've returned by now."

"Dace is missing too?" I glance at Calla. "When did they leave, Lily?"

"Dace left a while ago." Trent sits forward, gripping his knees with both hands. "I saw him head out. Going back to his ship, he said. I don't blame him—he was catching a lot of crap from everyone."

"Emie and Raid left soon after," says Lily. "Maybe they're all at the ship? I can run and check."

"No," says Calla. "I should return to the Ada anyway. You stay here—tell your parents that Ann and I will send the others back if we find them."

Lily frowns, looking just like her older sister. It occurs to me Emie might not be thrilled to see me. We'll have to sort that out sooner or later. "Yeah, you two stay here. We'll check it out."

Calla and I walk off, ignoring Trent and Lily's protests.

"Stubbornness seems a common trait on Eco," observes Calla, as we make our way to the back gate.

"They're probably pretty confused over this DNA thing." I glance over my shoulder to make sure the younger kids aren't following. "It's a shock, you know."

"I know about shock." Calla swings the gate open. "You get over it."

I eye her speculatively for a second. "Really?"

"No." Calla fastens the gate behind us and strides toward the Augusta Ada without looking at me again.

As we approach the cargo bay, a noise makes us both stop in our tracks. It's obviously human, though no words are distinguishable.

"Someone's in pain." Calla runs toward the far side of the ship.

I follow closely on her heels. As we round the back fins of the spacecraft, Raid stumbles out of the shadows.

There's blood caked on his lower lip and a violet bruise stains his left temple. He staggers toward us, slumping into the side of the ship a few feet from Calla.

She rushes to him and offers an arm to prop him up. "What the hell happened to you, kid?"

"Fight." Raid's voice cracks on the word.

I dash to his other side and slide an arm around his back, helping Calla keep him on his feet. "You okay? Who hit you?"

He gazes at me, his pupils slightly dilated. "Ann. Happy to see you. Thought maybe they'd grabbed you too."

There's a ball of acid rolling up the back of my throat. I want to slap whoever did this to him. Hard. "Your mom needs to take a look at this bump." I smooth the hair back from his temple with my free hand. "Wait a minute—grabbed me too? Who else did they grab?"

Raid straightens, pulling away from Calla's arm, though his body still rests against mine. "Dace and Emie. You need to do something." He stares into Calla's strange eyes. "Tell your captain, get some help … "

"Who took them?" Calla's gloved fingers slide across the butt of her laser pistol.

"Kam. His dad and uncle. A few others. Wanted Dace to show them the way to the caverns, where he found that mineral." Raid licks his lips and wipes the dried blood away with the back of his hand. "Knocked me out when I got in the way. Guess I was lucky they didn't shoot me."

Calla's fingers tighten on her pistol. "They have guns?"

"Yeah. Only way they got Dace to go. Threatened to hurt Emie." Raid looks down at me. "He's brave, the little scientist. I'll give him that."

I can't believe this. Emie and Dace, taken away at gunpoint? I lock my knees to prevent my legs from buckling. I clutch at Raid's shirt. "Kam wouldn't hurt Emie. He couldn't. He's in love with her … "

Black eyebrows disappear under the hair spilling over Raid's forehead. "She dumped him, remember? Anyway, it's Kam. He liked screwing around with her. But love? Not sure the guy knows what that is."

"Anything else? I mean, have any idea of their plan?" asks Calla.

"Well, they also had a sonic cannon. I saw it, and some explosives stuffed in the back of one of the rovers." Raid frowns. "I expect they plan to blast something at the cavern—try to open up the entrance maybe. Not sure."

Calla appears lost in thought. "Wait here. I'll be right back." She heads for the cargo bay.

Raid leans against the smooth metal hull of the ship. "Thought you'd be pissed at me."

"I was, for a while. But then I had time to think, and … I don't know. I guess I actually agree with what you and Dace did. Protecting the Selk, I mean." I keep my eyes down and focus on brushing some dirt from the sleeve of his shirt. "Even if it means exposing my secret."

"Our secret." Raid lays his hand over my moving fingers. "I've obviously got the same mutation, Ann. It's not like you're alone in this, you know."

Meeting his intense gaze, I curl my fingers around his hand. "I know."

"You should have seen Emie. She fought them off until Kam pulled the gun. But she got him good."

"Kneed him?"

"Right in the nuts." Raid's lips curl into a smile that quickly disappears when his cut opens and bleeds again. "Damn."

I reach up and wipe away the blood with my free hand. "Looks like you fought back too."

"For all the good it did."

"It did good." I stand on tiptoes and kiss him softly on the lips. "You did good."

Calla reappears, clutching something in her fist. "Okay, here's what I think. You two have a connection with those water creatures, right? Maybe you can warn them somehow?" She examines Raid. "That is, if you feel up to it."

"I can manage," Raid replies.

"So you do that while I round up some reinforcements. Your dad, Ann, and your grandparents … "

"My mother, Mia Lin." Raid straightens and steps away from the support of the ship. "She's a medic—could be useful."

"All right. And the captain, of course, and Jacobi. Anyone else?"

"Emie's parents—the Winstons. Ask my dad to grab a few

others." I release my hold on Raid's hand and meet his determined gaze. "Sure you feel like traveling anywhere?"

"I can do it. Emie's out there, and Dace. I'd rather do something, anything, than stand around here."

Calla holds out her hand. In her palm is a small bottle. "Take it. There are two pills inside. You each swallow one."

"What is it?" I take the bottle from her hand and hold it up to the light. Two tiny metallic balls roll around inside.

"Trackers." Calla shrugs. "Don't look surprised. Told you I was former military. This way, I can find either one of you, wherever you end up."

"Is it permanent?" Raid extends his hand.

I drop one of the pills into his palm. I tip the bottle and swallow the other.

"No." The faint hint of a smile twitches Calla's mouth. "It passes."

Raid grimaces, but pops the pill. "Nice," he says, wiping his mouth. He smoothes back his unruly hair before turning to me. "You know how to handle a rover? Not sure I should be driving."

"Sure. How hard can it be?" I plaster a smile on my face.

"Comforting." Raid taps my nose with one finger. "Oh well, I can talk you through it."

Calla reaches out and lays a hand on my arm. Her gloved fingers are surprisingly warm. "You two be careful. I wouldn't send you, but it'll take some time to gather a solid backup team, and I think somebody better warn those creatures as soon as possible."

"Not a problem," I say. Although, given Raid's battered

condition and my less than stellar fighting skills, I suspect we have a very big problem indeed.

But Kam and his crew might be planning something that could harm a lot of Selk. And they have Dace and Emie.

"Let's go." I take Raid's hand and pull him toward the small fleet of solar-powered vehicles. I've never driven a rover on my own, but it can't be much harder than riding a bike. I think.

"Meet you there," calls Calla. "With back-up. Stay safe!"

I tighten my lips and pick up speed to keep pace with Raid's longer strides. I really hope we can fulfill that last request.

CHAPTER TWENTY

I manage to maneuver one of the four-wheeled rovers over Eco's terrain with only a few pointers from Raid. It involves some shouting, but really, not too much instruction.

Raid spots the tracks of two other rovers. They lead directly toward the first cavern entrance. I veer away from the tracks, earning another barrage of shouts from Raid.

"Oh, shut up!" I spin the steering wheel sharply to dodge a large rock. "We don't want to just drive up on them, do we?"

Raid removes his hands from his temples to grip his knees. I'm sure the bumpy ride isn't doing his head any favors. I reach over to pat his arm.

"Hands on the wheel!" Raid shouts.

I shoot him a glare. "Who's driving?"

"Hell if I know." Raid braces one hand against the dashboard.

"Never seen you act so reckless before."

"Never had reason to." I focus on my surroundings. The rock pile that covers the first cavern lies off to our right, the entrance hidden by a dip in the landscape. I can just see light flash off the metal roll bars of one of the rovers. "Going around." I raise my voice to cut through the sound of rushing air. "Alternate entrance. Dace and I found it."

"When you went for that swim?" Raid's body is jolted into mine.

"Yeah." I spare him a quick glance. His left eye is swelling. "That kiss … "

"Never mind." Raid slides away from me, his words brighter than his expression. "I've kissed other people too."

I suspected as much, but hearing it stated so bluntly makes the muscles of my heart contract. "Well, sure." I lean forward, peering at the landscape before me while I studiously avoid Raid's eyes. "Anyway, we're almost there."

My foot hits the brake as I spy a circle of stones—the upper edge of the open-air pool where Dace and I discovered one of the Selks' food sources. The sudden stop slams Raid's knees into the dash.

He lets loose a colorful riff of popular obscenities.

"Sorry." I jump out of the rover. "Need any help?"

"No." Raid climbs out of the passenger side of the vehicle. "Safer without your assistance."

I add a few choice words of my own before taking his arm. "We have to climb down. Okay?"

Raid stares into the depths of the vegetation-clogged pool.

"Okay. But you walk behind me. If I fall, no use knocking you over too."

"Just hug the rock wall," I say, guiding him to the steep path that zigzags along one side of the natural well.

We make our way down, placing one foot in front of the other with a precision born of fear. I don't know if Raid's as terrified as I am, but I notice the blanched knuckles on the hand he slides along the rock wall.

Reaching the bottom, Raid expels a loud breath and slumps to the ground. "Now what?"

He looks terrible. The bruise glows purple against his skin, which has been drained of all its natural color. I kneel beside him. "Now we swim."

Raid narrows his good eye into a slit. The other eye is now almost closed. "Never mentioned swimming. Don't know how."

"Neither did I. All I'd ever done was play around with virtual sim stuff. I know you've done the same." I lightly rest my hands on his shoulders and examine his face. "But I can go by myself, if you want."

"Hell no." Raid brushes away my hands and struggles to his feet. "Where do we jump in? Here?"

"Uh, no. We can walk for a bit." I direct him toward the passage that leads to the second cavern. "There's another pool, further on. Bigger and not quite so … cluttered."

"That's good. Not looking forward to picking seaweed out of my teeth."

I swallow a laugh and pull a solar light from my emergency pack. "It's fresh water, loco mío."

"Save the lessons for later." Raid sticks close to my side as we move through the tunnel. "Hard to see."

I shine the flashlight and illuminate the trail before us. The path is strangely smooth, as if many pairs of feet have trod it before us. Is it only the bodies of the Selk that have polished these stones? I shiver, though it isn't cold in the corridor. "It's brighter up ahead."

"Good," says Raid, as we step into the larger of the two caverns.

A cluster of Selk rest on the bank. At our approach, they turn their dark eyes on us. There's interest, not fear, in their stares.

"Hello." Raid steps forward, holding out his hand.

The Selk rise, pressed up against one another in a solid wall of sleek brown fur and searching snouts.

Friends. I force the thought forward.

Raid's frozen in place, facing the barricade of Selk. I move close to his side. "Remember, let their thoughts flow over you. Don't fight it," I whisper, as I survey the numerous pairs of eyes watching us.

"Above."

The concept rings clear as a bell—a bell with a clapper that slams the inside of my skull. Out of the corner of my eye, I watch Raid clutch his head with both hands. But he, like me, remains on his feet.

"Yes, from above." I eye the Selk to see if this thought holds any meaning for them.

"Air. Light. Above."

I chase everything else from my thoughts. *"Yes, humans. From above."*

"Below. Water."

Despite my concerns, I feel a smile curve my lips. I sweep one hand before me to encompass the entire group of Selk. *"You. You live below, in the water."*

"Good. Above. Below."

Raid nods. He points one finger at the Selk, flips over his hand and taps his own chest. His lips move as he obviously sends forth a thought.

I place my hand on his other arm. "What are you saying?"

He gazes down at me, his good eye shining as dark and liquid as those of the Selk. "Us. I said 'us.'"

I stare into his battered face for a moment. "Us," I say aloud.

"Us." The thought reverberates through my whole body as one by one the Selk waddle forward to form a circle around Raid and me.

"Now," says Raid, taking hold of my hand. "We need to warn them."

I take a deep breath and close my eyes. Focusing on thoughts of danger, of the need to move, to flee, I feel as if time has stopped. There is no past, no future, only now. Only the desperate need to communicate with these strange, wonderful creatures. To tell them of the threats to their existence. To save them.

Raid's fingers tighten about mine. "I think they understand," he says softly. "Maybe, just maybe … "

A great tremor shifts the stone beneath my feet. "What the hell?"

"Blasting." Raid wheels about, facing the far wall of the cavern. "The other cavern is just beyond that wall?"

"Yes." The Selk slide to the lake edge and dive in, one after the other. I expect them to swim away, down one of their hidden passages, but instead their dark heads pop up, eyes fastened on us. They bob in the clear water, as if waiting.

Waiting for us to join them.

"Then we swim," says Raid.

***

We sit on two of the scattered boulders and yank off our footwear. I glance over at Raid. "Sorry 'bout Kam. I know he was your friend."

Raid tucks his socks into his boots. "We grew up together, and he was the only guy around my age. So yeah, we hung out. Not sure I'd call him a friend, though." He gives me a slight smile before turning his attention to tugging off his jeans. "You, I consider a friend. And Emie. Kam was more like someone you deal with because you have to."

"Never knew you felt that way." I shrug off my jacket, surreptitiously watching Raid. I'm mesmerized for a second by the sight of his long, well-muscled legs. "Anyway … " He stands, stretching his arms, and I look everywhere but at his face. "It's too bad Kam's gone off the deep end."

"He was always ready to blow at the slightest thing." Raid pulls his long-sleeved shirt over his head. He's wearing nothing but his T-shirt and boxers now.

I catch myself staring and shift my focus to the lake, where the Selk wait patiently. "You should leave your T-shirt on. Water's not really cold, but you're already shivering a bit."

"Might be shock." Raid's eyes focus on me like a laser as I slip off my jeans. "Or maybe excitement … "

"Feeling better, are you?" I move swiftly to the edge of the water, scooting on the stone ramp to slide into the lake. When I surface, Raid is watching me. "Well, get in, then. Work off some of that … energy."

"Just don't let me drown before I get to see that outfit wet."

"I make no promises." I tread water as two of the Selk circle me. "But these guys will keep you safe."

Raid grins, wincing slightly as he crosses to the water. After sliding down the stone ramp he grabs for one of the rocks edging the lake.

As Dace did for me, I give him a quick lesson. Just like me, Raid swiftly picks up the basic mechanics of swimming. Once he's moving easily, I take off. As my arms sweep through the water, I think of Dace saying I was half-fish.

Dace and Emie—where are they? Are they safe? I picture my friends with guns pressed against their foreheads and increase the force of my strokes.

Many of the Selk swim with us, circling to match our slower pace. When we reach the far wall the Selk dive and disappear, one after the other.

I lift my head. "Under," I instruct Raid, who looks nervous but dives anyway.

We surface on the other side of the wall. Raid sputters,

apparently having swallowed some water. He treads for a moment to catch his breath.

"Okay?"

"Fine." He glances around the chamber. "This is where we were before."

"Yes." I flip my braid, heavy with water, over my shoulder. "I'm heading for the shore."

Raid nods and sets off, his strong arms pulling him through the water with little need of assistance from his legs. I follow, flanked by several Selk.

When we reach the shoreline, I glance back and notice the water creatures have taken up positions at various points in the small lake. The gentle motion of their tails keeps them upright, their sleek heads held high above the surface.

I pull myself up and out of the water. Raid's already crouched on the rocky shore, shaking out his black hair. He lifts his head and stares at the rock-studded wall, where something shifts amid the shadows. He leaps to his feet and runs toward the moving object.

It's Emie and Dace, tied back to back. Strips of some material—it looks like the blouse Emie was wearing over her tank top the last time I saw her—are tied around their heads, covering their mouths.

I rush forward to pull the gag from Emie's mouth while Raid does the same for Dace.

"Outside," Dace croaks. "They've got explosives."

"We know." Raid fumbles with the knots in the ropes that bind Emie and Dace.

"Kam's gone nuts." Emie's wide eyes look like sunken black pools in her ashen face.

"Seems like it." I take her hand as Raid pulls the rope away. "Sorry you've had to deal with this alone. I should've been with you."

"No, better you weren't." Emie stands, leaning on me for support. "Dace and Raid tried to fight them off, you know."

I put my arm around her shoulders. "Heard you got a good jab in too."

A faint smile curls her lips. "Made him sing soprano."

Dace staggers to his feet. "Need to get out there and stop them." He examines Raid. "Have any weapons?"

Raid runs his hands down his torso. His wet shirt clings to his skin, outlining every rib and muscle. "On me? No."

"Me neither," I say, plucking my soaked tank top away from my body. "But Calla was rounding up reinforcements. They might be here already."

"How'd she know where to find us?" Dace looks from me to Raid and back again. "You provide directions?"

"Sort of," says Raid.

I give Emie a quick hug before pulling my arm away. "Why'd they tie you up in here? It would make more sense to keep you outside with them."

"Who says they're acting like they have sense?" Dace shakes out his legs and arms. "Told us that we'd be bargaining chips if anyone showed up to try to stop them. They plan to blast the cavern entrance. Want to widen it, they claim. Not sure why."

"You didn't hear that part." Emie runs her fingers through

her hair. "You were in the other rover. Kam said they'd set blasts that could trap us in the cavern if anyone tried to interfere. He was boasting about how his uncle knew all about explosives."

"But what's the point?" Dace looks genuinely puzzled. "So they open up the cavern entrance. Then what?"

Raid's expression turns solemn. "They need a wider entry." He motions toward the lake, where several Selk bob in the clear water. "They want to be able to drag one of the sonic cannons down here. Set it off and what do you think it might do?"

"Scare them?" Emie's gaze is focused on the lake. I realize it's her first experience of the Selk. Her face, its warm brown tones restored, mirrors the same wonder and joy Raid displayed when he first encountered the water creatures.

"Or kill them." Dace drums his fingers against his thigh. "That kind of weapon, using sound waves, could really hurt a creature like the Selk."

We all turn to stare at the lake. Several pairs of dark eyes stare back.

Friends, I think, sweeping my arm to include the four of us. *Friends. Good.*

I reach for Emie's hand as these thoughts ring through my head. She sinks to her knees, pulling me down beside her.

"Don't fight it," I whisper. "Let it ripple through you."

She nods and, with my help, stumbles back to her feet.

"It gets easier," says Raid, laying one hand on Emie's shoulder.

Dace looks wistful. "Wish I could hear it." He taps my arm. "Shouldn't we do something about Kam and the others? See if Calla is here, at least?"

I turn to him. His expression is a portrait of determination. "Good idea. Let's get you two out of here and see what's happening on the surface."

"Should we send the Selk away?" asks Raid.

"I've been trying to pass along that thought, but they seem determined to stay," I reply, with a quick glance at the lake. The Selk stare back at me, barely blinking.

Dace has already crossed to the path that leads out of the cavern. "Come on, let's get this sorted out," he calls, striding forward as a great blast shakes the cavern.

"Get down!" I scream, but it's too late. A cascade of rocks showers the path. One fragment hits Dace with a glancing blow, knocking him to the ground.

Raid's feet barely appear to touch the ground as he dashes to Dace's side. The clatter of stone hitting stone subsides. Emie and I reach Dace just as Raid sweeps the last of the rock fragments from his body.

Raid rests his ear against Dace's chest. "He's breathing." He sits back on his heels, stripping off his T-shirt. "Emie, come here and hold this against that cut on his head. Got to stop the bleeding."

The Selk make a high-pitched sound that scrapes my nerves like a file. I turn my head to see they have all gathered at the shoreline.

Alive. I concentrate all my energy on the thought. *He's alive.*

Their wails descend into a quiet keening.

I continue to stare at them, these alien creatures.

No, not so alien. *Us,* they claimed. We were different, our creation and development separated by space as well as species. But we shared things too. Enough to make our continued survival matter to both of us.

"Ann!" Raid's voice draws me back. "We need to get him help, but I'm afraid to move him without a medic checking him out first. If Calla followed our advice, if my mother's here, she can tell us what to do."

Dace looks so fragile, lying on the ground with one arm twisted at an odd angle. Crimson blossoms through the fabric Emie holds against his head. She looks up at me, her lips tightened in distress.

"Emie, you stay with him. We'll go for help." My voice sounds like it's emerging from someone else's throat. I squeeze my friend's shoulder. "The Selk can comprehend whatever you think, to a degree. If we give a signal—a shout or something— you tell them to flee. Just think 'flee' or 'escape' as hard as you can. Understand?"

She lifts her chin. "I'll do it, I swear. No matter what."

"Good." Raid leans in to kiss Emie on the cheek. "Kam never deserved you," he adds with a warm smile.

"No, he sure didn't." Emie strokes Dace's still hand. "Go on. I'll keep watch and listen for any signal."

I spare one last glance for Dace. His face has paled to the color of sand. "Raid—let's go put a stop to this."

"How?" Emie's voice quivers. I know the fear in her eyes isn't for herself. That knowledge makes me stiffen my spine and meet Raid's questioning eyes without hesitation.

"I don't know. But we'll do it. We have to."

CHAPTER TWENTY-ONE

We climb over fallen rock to reach the passage that leads outside. Raid, shirtless, collects several cuts on his torso, as well as his legs and arms. One sharp fragment scrapes the pad of my heel and I leave a trail of bloody footprints to the entrance. But for some reason, the pain barely registers.

The opening is wider than before. I shrink back against the stone wall of the passage to stay out of sight, then inch forward to peer around the corner. Raid moves in close behind me, his chest pressed so tightly against my shoulder I can feel his heartbeat.

"See anything?" he whispers in my ear.

"It's a standoff. Kam and his crew on one side, hunched behind their rovers; Calla, my family, and some others taking cover behind their own vehicles. Both sides pointing laser guns at each other." I turn my head to look up into Raid's face. "Your mom is here."

A spasm of anxiety twitches Raid's good eye. "We need her help with Dace. Does she have her med kit?"

"Looks like it."

"So we gotta step out there. Tell them what's up. Let me go first." Raid brushes past me. "Hopefully they won't shoot at anything that moves."

"Raid," I say, "you're not going anywhere without me." I take his hand in a firm grip.

He looks down at me. Even with his face marred by cuts and bruises, he still manages a seductive smile. "I like the sound of that."

We both exhale before stepping out into the light.

"Hold your fire!" my father's voice rings out.

I blink in the sunlight. Still holding Raid's hand, I clear my throat before raising my voice. "We need help. Dace is injured …"

Connor Patel jumps out from behind one of the rovers. Kam, who's cradling something in his palms, stretches out his hands.

"Stay put!" Kam waves one hand over his head. "I still have the detonator."

Patel freezes in place. "My nephew—he's never harmed you."

"Really?" Kam saunters into the buffer zone that separates the opposing groups. "He and his little investigations just closed Earth's doors to me."

"Would've been discovered anyway," says my grandmother.

I catch her eye. Her calm gaze steadies me. "Kam, Dace really does need help. Can we take Doctor Lin to him? Please?" I hate to beg Kam for anything, but this is Dace we're talking about.

I'd do anything for Dace. The thought slams against my skull like the voices of the Selk. I tighten my grip on Raid's hand. Dace and Raid. This could be a problem. But not one that matters right now.

"Kameron." My mother's honeyed tones immediately capture Kam's attention. "I'm sure you don't want Dace or anyone else to come to any real harm. Why not allow the doctor to take a look? The rest of us will stay here. As hostages, if you want."

My father lays a hand on Mom's shoulder. "Yes, you can keep us here. We'll even put down our weapons." He holds up his gun and tosses it out into the open space between the two sides. "Just permit Doctor Lin to check on Dace."

"And Emie?" Mr. Winston casts me a frantic look.

I lock my gaze with that of Emie's father. "Emie's okay. She's watching over Dace, but she's unharmed." Refocusing on Kam and his followers, I drop Raid's hand and step forward. "What do you say? Let the doctor take a look?"

Kam's fingers twitch, and a flash of fear crosses every face, even those in his own family. "Not the doctor. The colony can't afford to lose a medic. Someone else can check, but no funny business. I swear I'll blow those other charges if anyone pulls any crazy shit." His gaze sweeps over the group that includes my parents and grandparents. "Anyone else here know first aid?"

Calla steps forward, holding her gun over her head. "I do. Trained for basic emergency response in the military."

Kam studies the cyber for a second. "All right. Toss over your gun and grab the doc's med kit."

Calla carefully lowers her gun to the ground and kicks it toward Kam.

As Doctor Lin hands over the bag, she casts furtive glances at Raid, obviously concerned about his condition. Out of the corner of my eye, I see Raid mouth something at her. Reassuring her, no doubt.

I look back at my family. They're all staring at me, except for my mother, whose eyes remain fixed on Kam. I lift my hand and smile to indicate I'm fine.

"So, here's the deal." Kam turns to his uncle, swiftly swapping the detonator for a laser pistol. "My guys are going to keep you lot under surveillance. And Uncle's quite willing to blow those charges if anyone steps out of line."

Doug Frye's skin is the color of dough. He glances from his brother to his nephew before cradling the detonator close to his chest.

"I'm going to escort the cyber inside," continues Kam, pointing the gun at Calla. "Just to make sure these two are telling the truth." The pistol swings about to target Raid and me. "When we get back, we'll see about finishing this."

"We could finish it now if you'd listen to sense," says Mom. She walks right up to Kam.

I'm not the only one to gasp when he points the gun at her.

"Go ahead." Mom tosses her gleaming blonde hair. She's several inches shorter and many pounds lighter than Kam, but not one iota of fear shadows her face. "You think that will solve your problems, but it won't. The only thing that's going to help you now, Kameron Frye, is to put down that gun, tell your uncle to lay down the detonator, and all of you—just walk away."

Kam presses the barrel of the pistol against Mom's forehead.

"You need to back off."

Mom lifts one slender hand, but instead of pushing aside the gun, she lays her fingers on Kam's wrist. "Really, Kameron, this is so melodramatic." She strokes his arm. "Drop the gun, please, and I will walk back to join my family. We don't want to destroy our friendship do we?"

Kam's eyes appear glazed. He lowers the pistol. Mom takes the opportunity to back up, step by step, until she bumps into Connor Patel who's rushed forward to meet her. He wraps his arms tightly around her. I glance at my dad; he's staring at his boots.

"Okay, then. Get a move on." Kam wheels around to face Raid and me. "You," he motions toward Calla, "walk in front of me—behind those two."

"One moment." My grandfather strips off his jacket. "Can I toss this to Raid? He looks cold."

Kam stares at Raid. "Yeah, what's up with the half-naked thing, dude? Took a moment out of your rescue operation to screw Solano?"

"We were swimming," replies Raid calmly, his teeth chattering. It is colder outside than in the caverns, and what little clothes we're wearing are still damp.

"Throw it over here," Kam instructs Grandfather. When the jacket sails to his feet, Kam snatches it up and searches its pockets before tossing it to Raid.

"Put it on and move out." Pointing the pistol toward the cavern entrance, Kam waits until Calla falls in behind Raid and me before striding forward. "Remember, I'm still back here, and

I'm the one holding the gun."

"Yeah," mutters Raid, as he follows me to the entrance. "Real brave, asshole."

I shush him and lead the way into the passage. With the entrance blasted open, it's brighter than before, but I still keep one hand on the wall to guide my way down. "Watch for falling rock," I call over my shoulder just as a chunk of Dace's mineral splits off the ceiling and crashes at my feet.

"Shut up and walk," says Kam.

I share a glance with Raid. There are three of us—four, once we reach the first cavern—and one of Kam. He has a laser gun, but …

Raid nods, as if reading my mind. He taps my shoulder. "When we're inside," he whispers.

"No talking!" yells Kam.

The large chamber opens before us, the light from the shafts piercing the shadows. We pick our way over a barrier of stones to take the path down to the shore.

Emie's sitting by Dace's still body. She looks up at our approach, her joy turning to fear when she spies Kam.

"Don't worry," Raid calls out, "we've brought help."

I gaze out over the lake. The Selk have submerged for the moment, but their dark forms are clearly visible swirling through the water. As we reach the bottom of the path, I catch Kam staring at the lake.

His expression radiates suspicion. "What's moving in there?"

"The Selk, of course." I walk toward the water's edge.

"Stop," commands Kam. "No communication with your

alien friends."

I feel a giggle rise in my throat. Stupid time, bad place, but Kam's so right he's wrong … The giggle erupts in a peal of laughter.

"You nuts?" Kam strides forward and grabs me by the arm. He jerks me around to face him.

"Hey!" Raid moves in, his fists raised.

Calla steps between him and Kam. "Enough. We're here to help the kid."

"Right." Raid glares at Kam, who drops my arm but keeps his gun trained on us.

"How's he doing?" I ask Emie.

"No better, no worse." Emie's dark eyes are shadowed under her lowered eyelids.

Whatever you think … I know what she's doing. A very smart girl, as my father said.

My foot's throbbing, but I push the pain aside. "Can we go to him?" I ask Kam.

He gives a curt nod. "You and the cyber. Raid can stay here and keep me company."

Calla and I make our way to Dace. Kneeling, I place my arm around Emie's shoulders. "You want to get up and stretch for a minute?" I whisper.

"Still thinking," she replies, with a little tip of her head toward the lake.

I pat her arm and turn my attention to Dace. "How is he?"

Calla, focused on examining Dace's head injury, doesn't look up. "He'll live. Nasty cut, though."

"He's been out quite a while." I take one of Dace's hands. It feels cool, but not limp. "Sure that's okay?"

"Probably better than thrashing about." Calla rummages through the med kit for some antiseptic and a bandage.

Kam's pistol is still trained on Raid, but the redhead keeps sneaking glances at the lake. Obviously, the Selk are affecting him in some way, which might mean he can be easily distracted. "Do you think … ?"

Calla looks up at me, her strange eyes unreadable. "Four to one. Yeah, I've thought it. But only after I fix up the kid. Next thing is a splint for that arm. Might need your help."

I move around to the other side of Dace's prone body and hold his arm at the proper angle for the splint.

"You 'bout done?" asks Kam. He's shifting his weight from foot to foot.

"Almost," says Calla.

I catch Raid's eye. "Four to one," I mouth, when Kam glances once more at the lake.

Raid nods. I walk over to Emie and kneel beside her. "Be ready to take him down," I say in her ear.

"No whispering!" Kam shoves the barrel of the gun into Raid's back. Forcing Raid to walk in front of him, Kam crosses to us. "Get up, Solano!"

I stand, helping Emie to her feet. "Just discussing Dace's condition."

"Over there." Kam jerks his head toward a shallow indentation in the cave wall. "Stand over there." He gives Raid a shove. "You too."

As we move toward the wall, Kam pushes Calla aside and leans over Dace. "Not done yet? He looks okay to me."

"I was going to try to wake him." Calla's voice is perfectly calm. She reaches into the med kit and pulls out a small vial. "Mind?"

"Nah, go ahead. Might be easier to get him out under his own steam."

Calla stares at Kam for a moment. "Right." She kneels and waves the vial under Dace's nose.

His eyelashes flutter and his good hand reaches up to swat at the vial. "Wah-h-h … " He sputters and coughs, then attempts to lift himself.

He groans and flops back, but not before Calla throws her arm around him to keep his head from hitting the stones.

"Careful," she says, easing him into a sitting position. "You've had a nasty head injury and banged up one arm. Don't try to move too fast."

Kam sweeps the pistol from side to side, taking in all of us. "Get him on his feet."

Calla stands in one graceful motion. "He was knocked out. He's just come to, and you want to march him out of here?" That artificial face, perfectly composed, and yet—there's a look in her eyes that raises the hair on my arms. Without a word, she leans over and gently lifts Dace to his feet.

"Lean on me," she tells him.

"See—he's standing. Good. We can't waste all day in here." Kam gazes about the chamber. "That mineral—it's everywhere. Right here, ready for the diggers … "

The lake erupts in a flurry of splashes. Kam's entire body jerks as he spins to stare at the water. The gun flies from his fingers and clatters to the rocky ground.

"On my signal," whispers Raid, taking my hand.

I reach for Emie's fingers. "Ready."

Like a dark army materializing from the mist, the Selk rise from the lake. Kam shrieks—a strange, strangled sound that is instantly matched by the voices of the Selk.

Friends. No harm.

The thoughts wash over me. My grip tightens on both Raid's and Emie's hands. Fingers entwined, we lean back against the support of the stone wall. I realize there's no need for us to take any action now.

No harm. Protect.

Kam has fallen to his knees, his pistol kicked to the side, forgotten. He covers his ears with his hands and rocks back and forth, screaming.

Friends. Above. Protect.

Thank you. I repeat the thought over and over, hoping the Selk will understand. *Thank you. Friends.*

Unaffected by the water creature's thoughts, Calla and Dace stand side by side, Calla's arms wrapped around Dace to keep him on his feet. They stare at the Selk, Dace with a faint smile and Calla with her mouth opening and closing like a trap.

"Oh my God." Calla's voice catches like a broken gear. "It's them."

CHAPTER TWENTY-TWO

The Selk's voices fade away at Calla's words. Kam, released from the mental battering produced by the water creatures' communication, looks around frantically for a second and lunges for his discarded pistol.

Leaping forward at the same time, Raid's foot makes contact with the weapon just as Kam's fingers touch the barrel, kicking the gun away with enough force to send it skittering over the rocky ground and into the lake.

"Son of a bitch!" Kam makes a grab for Raid's ankle but Raid's swinging foot knocks him aside.

Calla shoots me a swift glance, and I run to her side to support Dace.

"Lean on me," I tell him.

He looks at me, his pupils still dilated. "Hanging on as tight as I can."

Emie dashes forward to help me keep Dace on his feet as Calla strides over to Kam and Raid.

"Get up, dirt-treader." She pokes Kam with her boot. "Don't expect you're quite so dangerous without a weapon. Now me," that strange smile splits her face, "I've been trained to use my fists quite expertly."

Kam stands slowly, his eyes fixed on Calla. "I'm not going to be anyone's prisoner. Definitely not some shitty cyber's."

"Start swimming then, because you aren't getting out of here the other way—unless you follow my instructions." Calla motions for Raid to join her. "In my pocket is some 'lastic. Grab it and help me tie up this asshole's hands, would you?"

Raid grins and gives Calla a swift salute. "Happy to comply, commander."

I adjust my grip around Dace's back, allowing him to slouch into my supporting arm. My fingers brush Emie's hand as she mirrors my action. We share an encouraging smile behind Dace's back.

"You'll be sorry," Kam mutters.

"Well, you're already sorry," says Calla, earning another grin from Raid. She examines Raid's handiwork as he binds Kam's hands. "Now then, trussed up like a proper package. Guess you'll be the one marching to orders this time, dirt-treader."

"Don't call me that!" Kam spits the words through gritted teeth. He levels a glare at Emie. "There's the little traitor. Should've known she'd be easily swayed, what with being so free and loose with her body."

Calla studies him for only a second before she smacks him,

hard, across the mouth. He staggers back, falling against Raid's crossed arms.

"Say anything like that again," Raid says, leaning in to speak directly into Kam's ear, "and I will hit you too. And it won't be a smack, trust me." He thrusts Kam forward.

Calla closes her gloved fingers over Kam's bound wrists and spins him around. "Now, stand here until I tell you to move. Better yet, let's shut that yap of yours." She marches over to the medical bag and pulls out a roll of gauze. Over Kam's vehement protests, she gags him with the gauze. As she finishes tying it off, she glances over his shoulder. "What's that?"

"The Selk." Dace's voice is gaining strength. "They've brought up the gun."

I'm mesmerized by the activity in the lake. The Selk are tossing the pistol back and forth like a toy ball. Seemingly tired of their game, one creature sweeps its large tailfin over the water just as the gun hits the surface. The pistol shoots up and sails over the lake, smashing against the closest wall. The sound of metal hitting stone reverberates through the cavern as bits of the gun fly off in all directions, sparking like embers from a fire.

The Selk bob in the water, watching this display with interest. As the broken weapon slides to the bottom of the lake, the creatures turn, one by one, and swim toward the far wall. They dive and disappear.

Calla stares blankly at the empty lake. "There's another cavern," I tell her. "You just have to swim under."

"What you said before—what did you mean?" Dace takes a step toward Calla, forcing Emie and me to move with him.

Kam gnaws at his gag to no avail. Raid grips Kam's shoulder to hold him in place as we wait for Calla's reply.

"I've seen them before," Calla says, sweeping her gaze over all of us. "Those creatures. On Shenlong."

"That's on the other side of the galaxy." Dace straightens, pulling away from Emie's arm. "Must've been something similar, not the actual Selk. I mean, they're pretty smart, but I can't see them constructing and flying spacecraft."

"Looked just like them." Calla's expression is implacable. "Sounded just like them, too. Although they weren't living underground on Shenlong. Found them in surface rivers, actually. Strange thing is … " Calla glances back at the water. "We were doing a survey, you see, during one of my military tours. Documenting and cataloging stuff. Found creatures just like your Selk. They seemed well-adapted to the environment, but the biologist types said they weren't native to the planet."

Dace blinks rapidly, his eyelashes fluttering like moths' wings. "They were brought there?"

"Dunno," Calla replies with a shrug. "That was the idea I got, but nobody ever figured it out." She glances back at the lake. "There was something about them, those creatures, that made you feel good. Calm and happy. Lots of the crew spent more time with them than they needed to. Me included."

"You really think it's the same species?" Dace raises his injured arm then groans and slumps against me.

"I'd swear to it." Calla looks him up and down. "Now—we gotta get you out of here. You need more medical attention."

"I'm okay." Dace's face is blanched the color of bone.

"Sure you are," I say. "You look like shit, Keeling."

"At least I'm not half-naked, Solano." He manages a faint smile.

"You saying I look like shit when I'm half-naked?" I throw out the response without thought. One glance at Raid's face and I realize I've crossed a line. I adjust my hold on Dace.

He grimaces. "No, I … that's not what I meant … "

Oh, to hell with the line. I lean in and kiss his pale cheek. "I know."

Raid moves to Dace's other side and shoots me one sharp look before turning his attention to Dace. "Here, let me help. It'll take both of us to get him over those rocks strewn on the path. Probably hurt like hell," he adds, sliding Dace's good arm around his shoulders. "Apologizing in advance."

"I can handle it." Dace takes a few steps and presses his lips together, but not before a strangled sound escapes.

"Emie," I call out. "Got any pain meds in that bag?"

"Checking." She rummages through the med kit and pulls out a small foil packet. "This work?"

Raid spares the packet a quick glance. "That'll do."

We pause as Emie extracts the pills and pops them onto Dace's tongue while Calla marches Kam forward, her fist jabbing the small of his back.

Kam jerks his head from side to side, trying to dislodge the gag. His eyes flash with rage. After one more shove from Calla, he throws a foot back, slamming a kick into her shin. She yelps and stops in place, allowing Kam to veer to the right. He staggers toward the wall that rises below the inclined pathway.

"Hey!" Raid lowers Dace's full weight onto me, buckling my knees. Emie drops the medical bag and rushes to help me support Dace while Raid strides toward Kam and Calla.

Working to free his hands, Kam stumbles, slamming his shoulder into the wall. Calla is only a step or two behind him. A moment of silence, of dust rising in the air and drifting back down, is followed by a thunderous crack. Calla looks up, lifting her gloved hands amid a shower of black and silver dust.

High above our heads, a piece of the stone ceiling trembles and splinters.

And sheers off.

Calla throws her body at Kam, hitting him with so much force he slides along the wall for a moment before tumbling to the ground.

A chunk of stone hurtles to the base of the cavern like a spent meteor and pins Calla to the floor.

When the dust settles, only the cyber's head and one hand are visible. The rest of her body is buried under a boulder, the large rock still in one piece even though its surface is crazed with fissures.

I hear the sound of gasping and wheezing long before I realize it's coming from my own throat.

Emie cries soundlessly, tears spilling down her cheeks and dripping from her chin. Kam lies to one side, just out of range of the massive stone, his green eyes wide with horror.

"Sit me down!" Dace pulls against Emie's hands and my arm. "Go to her!"

We gently lower Dace to the ground, propping him against the bottom of the inclined path, and race to Calla.

Raid, already there, kneels by her free hand. He looks up at me and shakes his head. He slips off her leather glove, picks up Calla's hand, and strokes those cold metal fingers. She probably can't feel it, but I guess it doesn't matter. I suppose at this point the only thing that matters is that he can.

Emie kneels beside Raid and I crouch down by Calla's head. Her eyes are open, her lips moving. I wipe the dampness from my face and lean in to hear what she's saying.

"One more time," she croaks. "Saving one more dumb-ass." Those strange eyes roll up to look into mine then over at the lake. "Oh. Hello."

I follow her gaze. A solitary Selk has returned. Its dark eyes are even moister than usual, almost as if it were weeping.

Surely these creatures don't cry. I rub the tears from my own eyes. The Selk holds our gazes for a moment, then turns away. It leaps higher than I've ever seen one jump, shedding water from its sleek fur in a shower of droplets that reflect the light like tiny prisms. Diving back down, it flips its body one full turn before breaking the surface of the water.

It's beautiful and somehow solemn, like a salute. I turn back in time to see Raid reaching to close Calla's eyes.

The silence stretches like a fast-growing vine, broken only by Emie's snuffling and Kam's boots kicking against the stone floor.

"We need to get out of here," Dace's hoarse voice echoes through the cavern. He points at the ceiling. "The charges have obviously destabilized this section."

Five pairs of eyes look upward. Above our heads, the rocks that comprise the roof of the cavern creak, shifting ever so slightly.

A fine dust sifts down on our bodies.

Raid jumps to his feet, strides over to Kam, and yanks the knot from his gag. "You," he says, pulling the gauze from Kam's mouth, "need to help me carry Dace out of here. Will you do it?" Raid's arms hang loosely at his sides, but his fingers are clenched into fists.

"I will." Kam raises his bound hands. "But you'll need to cut me loose."

The two boys, whom I've seen together so often, and thought such close friends, face off like rival warriors.

"If you promise to cause no more trouble."

"I swear," says Kam. "Just want to get out of here alive."

Raid waves his hand at Emie. "Bring over the med kit, would you?"

She hurries over to him, bag in hand. "Scissors?" She pulls a pair from the bag. "Or a knife?"

"Scissors will do." Raid sets about cutting through the 'lastic while Emie watches, fingering the handle of a gleaming surgical blade.

With one last glance at Calla's still face, I cross to Dace. "You hanging in there?"

"Sort of," he says. "But we shouldn't linger. Really." His face is streaked with tears.

"She was brave," I say, crouching beside him. "She saved Kam, even though he didn't deserve it."

"A human impulse." Dace's dark eyes search my face. "Even if the laws claim she wasn't exactly human."

"Those laws are crap." I realize how deeply I mean this as the words leave my mouth. "Total crap."

Dace's full lips curve into a faint smile. "Now you sound like Emie."

"Not a bad thing." I stand and meet Emie's determined face as she, Raid, and Kam approach. "Being more like Emie is a compliment."

"For sure," says Dace, giving my friend a smile that makes her stop in her tracks.

I look from Emie to Dace. Okay, so maybe I shouldn't worry so much about choosing between Raid and Dace. I may not be the only girl Dace finds interesting. This thought slams into my head almost as hard as the Selk's silent communications.

"Time to go," says Raid, as another drift of dust showers us. He leans over to assist Dace to his feet. "Kam, help me. Between the two of us, we should be able to lift him over those rocks."

Kam obeys without a word. He and Raid link arms to form an impromptu chair while Emie assists me in making sure Dace is securely cradled in their arms. As they carry Dace toward the inclined path, Kam casts a final glance back at the stone burying Calla's body.

She saved his life. Even though she didn't love him—didn't even like him. She saved him because it was the right thing to do. Because she could.

"Emie," I say as we scramble over the fallen stones on the path, "I think I'd like to help you with that mission of yours."

She pauses, catching her breath. "To defeat the genetics laws? To open Earth to the cybers and others?"

"That's the one," I say, as we turn the corner and walk toward the bright light that lies beyond the passage.

CHAPTER TWENTY-THREE

Connor Patel runs toward us, ignoring Kam's uncle and the detonator clutched to his chest.

"Dacian!" Connor reaches out with both hands as Raid and Kam set Dace on his feet. "Are you all right?"

"I'll be okay." Dace sways slightly.

"I was so worried … " Connor pulls Dace into an embrace. After a moment, he pushes his nephew back, still holding onto his shoulders. Lifting one hand, he brushes Dace's thick hair away from his forehead. "That's quite a bump. You need medical attention."

Emie holds up the med kit and Mia Lin rushes forward. While Raid's mother checks out Dace, my mom and dad step out from the cluster of people gathered behind the rovers.

"So—everyone else is okay?" asks Dad, examining me with concern.

"We're fine." I move into his proffered hug. The feel of his strong arms around me is more comforting than any words.

As if freed from a stun beam, Emie runs to her parents while Raid moves to his mother's side. Dad kisses my forehead before he releases me. I watch Kam stride over to his uncle and father.

"Disarm it," he says. "We're done here."

His father wordlessly grips Kam's hand and Doug Frye exhales a gusty sigh, switching off the detonator. He hands the small box to Kam, who stares at it for a moment before tossing it to the ground.

"We're done," he says again, and smashes the dead detonator under his boot. He turns to face the colonists who opposed him. "You can take us in, now."

No one moves. Finally, my mother takes a few steps toward Kam and his supporters. "This is a matter for the Council. Go back to the compound." She casts a commanding glare upon all present. "No one will harm you."

As she finishes speaking there's a roar—a cascade of rock sliding and crashing upon rock. Everyone stares at the cavern entrance, now blocked by a tumble of great stones. Dust rises from the rocks like smoke from a dying fire.

Connor Patel, his arm about Dace's shoulder, glances from Kam to me, Raid, and Emie, and back to Kam again. "Wait. Where's Calla?"

I take a deep breath, but before I can speak Raid steps forward and tells the others of Calla's sacrifice. His words are simple and straightforward, but when he stops talking tears slide down several cheeks.

I look at my mother. Her eyes are dry, but there's a curious look on her face. Almost as if she is, for once, uncertain. Almost.

"Ann," she says, moving to take my hands. "You and your friends have been very brave. But now we must get back to the colony." She glances at Kam and his group. "Things must be decided."

I grip her fingers—perhaps a little too tightly. Her golden eyebrows arch up over those beautiful eyes. "You need some rest, my dear," she says, giving my arm a little pat. "And some more clothes, perhaps?"

We must explain, then, where and why Raid and I discarded our other clothing.

My dad and grandparents propose to go and recover our rover.

"We can also climb down into that other cavern to find your boots and such, if you want," offers my father.

"You may encounter the Selk," I tell my grandmother when she slips in close enough to give me a fierce hug.

"Could prove quite exciting," she replies. "I think I'm up for it."

"You're always up for anything." I press a swift kiss to her cheek. "But be careful."

She tweaks the tail of my braid. "I've dealt with far greater dangers for more years than you've been alive, nieta."

"And conquered all," says Grandfather. He grins as he evades Grandmother's slap at his arm. "You're quite a bit like her, you know." He throws his arm around my shoulder and pulls me close.

"Am I?" I gaze up into his dark eyes. "Really?"

"Mucho. Sometimes when I look at you, I see her when we first met. And the same stubborn, glorious spirit … " Grandfather coughs and releases me. "Now—off you go with your mom. We'll meet you back at the compound."

I nod and follow my mother to one of the rovers. Raid and his mom are already inside, bracing Dace between them.

"No room." I back away as Connor Patel jumps in the front seat next to my mother who—no surprise—is driving.

"Sure there is," says Raid, flashing me a grin. "There's my lap."

He looks so odd—one eye closed to just a slit, the purple bruise discoloring the skin from his left temple down his jawline—and yet, there's that devilish smile. As if none of it matters. As if he's still just as handsome as ever.

I have to admire that confidence. That lack, if I really think about it, of ego.

"It might be a bumpy ride. You'll have to hang onto me." I climb into the back seat and settle on his lap.

"Not a problem." He wraps his arms around me, accidentally elbowing Dace in the process.

I catch Dace's eye. He smiles wanly and gives a little jerk of his head toward Raid.

"Boyfriend," he mouths silently at me. Fortunately Raid's distracted by something on the horizon.

"Friend," I say quite firmly, and out loud. "Who's a boy."

"Hey!" Raid tightens his grip. "What're you two talking about?"

"Oh, nothing," I say, patting Raid's bare knee.

Dace doesn't speak, but I catch a smile spreading over his face before he lowers his head to examine his splinted arm.

**

Our medical clinic appears deserted except for Mia Lin, who's slumped over a desk in the front room. Her head rests upon her crossed arms, her dark hair veiling her face.

I tiptoe past her. No sense in waking her—she's earned her rest. Once we returned to the compound, she set about checking those of us who were in the cavern, even Kam. Of course, most of her attention was focused on Dace's concussion. Not surprising that he has one, but a concern.

I know Dace is resting in one of the tiny exam rooms despite his uncle's protests that he'd be better off on the ship. Mia Lin and Boris, the other colony medic, had prevailed, arguing that since the Augusta Ada's best first-aid officer was no longer available, Dace had better stay at the clinic for observation. At least overnight.

I frown, remembering how this mention of Calla silenced Connor Patel.

Slipping though the half-open door, I spy Dace in one of the clinic's narrow beds. He's lying on his back, his face turned to the ceiling, eyes closed. Boris, who's leaning against the corrugated metal wall, puts a finger to his lips as I move close to the bed.

"Can I sit with him for a bit?" I whisper. "Give you a break. I'll call you immediately if I think he needs help."

Boris looks me up and down before nodding in reply. "Immediately," he mutters as he walks by me. "Be right outside."

"Of course." I wait for the medic to leave before pulling the room's lone chair closer to the bed.

Dace's eyes fly open. "He's gone?"

"Yes, but you're supposed to be sleeping."

"Too much on my mind." Dace tilts his head to look at me. "Where'd you go, after we got back? Saw Raid's mom check you over, but then you guys were out the door."

His damaged arm is now encased in a soft plastic pressure cast; his other arm is draped limply over his chest. I press my fingers over his good hand and feel the steady thump of his heart.

"Raid and Emie and I—we went to the rec hall to talk to the other kids. Raid rounded them up. He's pretty good at that."

"Like the Pied Piper," mutters Dace.

"What's that?"

"Oh, old Earth story. You never heard it?"

"No." I stare at Dace's face for a second. His eyes are half closed, but I sense he's watching me closely. "Anyway, we talked to all the colonists between the ages of ten and twenty, or thereabouts. Wanted to give them the real story—about Promissium, but also the Selk. And what the mining might do, for good or bad. Wanted to see what they thought."

"What was the consensus?"

"Well … " Keeping my fingers curled about his, I pull Dace's hand closer to the edge of the bed. "It was weird. Raid talked about the Selk and how he felt around them. That we needed to protect them somehow. And Emie brought up the whole business of the genetic purity laws and how none of us would probably be allowed to travel to Earth anyway. And I … "

"You?" Dace gazes at me from under those impossibly thick lashes. "What did you say, Ann?"

I cover our joined fingers with my other hand and draw them to my chest, pressing them over my heart. "I said I'd realized, finally, that Eco was my home. No—our home. And I wasn't about to let our home be destroyed just so we could collect a few credits."

"So—no mining? What about the benefits of Promissium?" Unless I'm mistaken, there's a sparkle of devilment in Dace's dark eyes. "Not that I want the Selk harmed, you understand. But scientifically … "

"Hah! See, even you're torn." I lower our clasped hands to the bed.

"I am. I admit it." Dace examines me, his lower lip rolling out into that familiar pout. "But you've a suspiciously smug look about you, Ann Solano. I think you have more to tell me."

"That's the great part!" I don't realize I've raised my voice until Boris pokes his head in.

"We're fine." Dace waves him aside.

"Should be sleeping … " Boris' voice trails off as he walks away.

"Great part?" Dace clenches my fingers tighter.

I squeeze back. "Hang on, I'm getting there." Straightening in the chair, I lift my chin and look down my not inconsiderable nose at him—with any luck, just as my grandmother would. "You, Dacian Keeling, are looking at one of the most brilliant people on Eco."

"One of? Not *the*?"

"Oh, now, I can't claim that. There's Emie, you know. And my family. And … " I can't keep a grin from spreading over my face, " … you're here."

He laughs—a loud, full-bodied guffaw. We have to wave Boris off again before we can continue talking.

"Anyway, the thing is—Raid and Emie led the discussion, but as they were talking, it occurred to me maybe there was another way to handle the situation. So I made a proposal, and everyone immediately jumped all over it. They're going to take it to their parents and the other adults this evening."

"Way to drag out the suspense. This isn't story hour, you know." Dace releases my hand and grabs the opposite bed rail. "So what's the deal?" He struggles to pull himself into a sitting position.

As I lean in and adjust his pillows to prop him up, he uses his good hand to draw me close. "Spill."

I stare into those dark eyes. Not only beautiful, but also brimming with intelligence. "Well, we've decided we *will* mine Promissium, but not on a grand scale. We'll do it manually, or with light equipment. Just take a bit here and there, from all the caves we can find. That way, we can all collect some extra credits and share the mineral with those that need it without destroying the Selk's habitat."

"And who's going to do this mining?" Dace's lips are only inches from mine.

I turn my head and stare at a blank holo monitor mounted on the wall. "Everyone. All on Eco who are able. We'll take shifts so no one has to do too much. Raid thinks we can collect enough to make it profitable, even if we each only spend a couple of hours a week on the project."

"Ingenious."

"Well, we don't know if the other colonists will agree, but it seems like a great compromise. I mean, it helps everyone, and since we can't jet off to Earth anyway … "

"Yet." Dace tugs on my sleeve, forcing me to look at him. "You're going to help Emie with her campaign, aren't you?"

"Yes. Maybe I can't go to a major university, but I can do the virtual equivalent using holodiscs and the 'sphere. Learn all I can about social systems, and politics, and the law, and then … " I meet his brilliant gaze and hold it, " … work to change things."

"Sounds like a plan." A smile twitches Dace's lips. "You and Emie—the powers-that-be don't have a chance."

"It'll take time."

"So will my studies. But that's something we both have, I hope—time."

"Yeah." I study his face for a moment. "So you're definitely leaving with your uncle?"

"Have to. That degree's even more essential now. Might be other creatures like the Selk who need protection."

"You'll be back, though? To study the creatures on Eco, I mean?"

"Sure. Every chance I get. Breaks and holidays. I have a lot more research to conduct on the Selk." He tips his head to one side, examining me as if I were one of his alien species. "And you know, I might need some more lessons before I'm ready to tackle those university girls."

I unsuccessfully attempt to swallow a chuckle. "You're not supposed to tackle them, exactly … "

"See—you've already helped." He flashes a bright, toothy grin before continuing in a more serious tone. "I know Raid's here. And he's pretty awesome—even I can admit that. So I'm not expecting anything. But I want us to be friends."

"I don't have a problem with that." I return his careful appraisal. "We can holo chat every now and then, although don't expect too much—sometimes our communication system craps out for months at a time. But there's messaging, too."

"Still good. Keep in touch. Only … " Dace strokes one finger across the back of my hand. "It's not quite like being in physical proximity."

"Physical proximity?" I raise my eyebrows. "Okay, Professor, another little tip, free of charge—drop that kind of talk if you want to interest a girl. Be a bit more informal."

"Like this?" Dace takes hold of my hand and pulls me in for a kiss.

It's a nice kiss. No, better than that.

It's a kiss that flips everything, that fills my head with confusion again.

"Damn, who have you been practicing on?" I make sure to keep my tone light.

Dace grins again. "No one. Just allowed myself the freedom to be a little more informal."

"Huh." I sit back. We stare at each other for a full minute before I find my voice. "So, that stuff Calla said about the Selk. Are you going to investigate that as well?"

"If I can convince Uncle to take me to Shenlong, sure." Dace rests against the pillows, his eyes never leaving my face. "It is weird such similar creatures would pop up on distant planets. I suppose it's possible, if you take into account the theory of convergent evolution … Oh, sorry. I'm being too pedantic again, aren't I?"

"'Fraid so." I make a mental note to look up "pedantic." "Anyway, Calla claimed the creatures on Shenlong weren't native to the planet. That means, what?"

"They were transported there."

"But by whom?"

"Or what?" Dace smiles. "It's fun, huh? Exploring, discovering new things. Keeps life interesting."

"Yeah." I lean in and adjust his pillows so his body slips down and he ends up flat on his back. "Now, you're supposed to be sleeping. Boris is gonna throw me out if we keep talking."

"I'll shut up, then." Dace looks up at me. "I don't want you to go. Will you stay with me awhile?"

"Sure, but do you mind if I sit on the edge of the bed? This chair's hard as those rocks in the cavern."

"No problem," says Dace, moving over as I settle onto the bed. "You can even lie down if you want."

"Hmmm … I think I'll just lean back on one of these extra pillows, thanks."

There's definitely a mischievous glint in Dace's dark eyes.

"What's the matter, Ann? Don't trust yourself?"

I stare at him for a moment, my lips pulled tight. "Now get this straight, Dacian Keeling. I have no intention of giving you any more lessons. And certainly ... " the smile escapes despite my attempt to smother it, " ... not until you have both hands available."

Dace's laughter draws Boris back. The medic just stares at us and mutters something about "kids" before shaking his head and walking away.

CHAPTER TWENTY-FOUR

In just a few hours, the Augusta Ada will blast off Eco. Standing in our tiny, unattractive, living space, I watch my father scramble eggs.

"You should go and say goodbye," he tells me, without turning around.

He's talking about Mom, of course. She sent word by Grandfather that she's in the lab, gathering up the last of her things. After the Council decided to follow my plan for mining Promissium on a small scale, she moved her belongings into the lab. I don't know if she's been sleeping there or on the ship with Connor Patel, but I've decided it doesn't matter. She's leaving, and my father's apparently made his peace with that. Or so he tells me.

"Not sure I want to." I pad over to the microstove and lean into his back, wrapping my arms around his waist.

"Careful, chica. Don't want to splatter," he says, but reaches up one hand to pat my arm.

"Sure you're okay?"

"I'm fine." Dad lays down his plastic spoon and turns off the burner with a wave of his hand. "Want some eggs?"

"No thanks." I release him and step back.

He turns around, allowing the eggs to congeal in the pan. His brown eyes study me with the intensity he uses to examine engineering diagrams. "Now—what's this I hear about Kam traveling on the Ada? You know what's up with that?"

"Captain Patel made a deal with him or something. He has to replace Calla … " I take a breath. "Anyway, he'll be another pair of hands. And it's better than him staying here with everyone watching him all the time."

"Makes sense. Good of Patel to offer." Surprisingly, there's no trace of rancor in Dad's voice. "Of course it'll be rough work, but it is probably better if Kam stays off Eco for a while. The rest of his family, and the others who helped them, are going to be under surveillance for some time."

"I imagine so." I fiddle with my braid. "I really don't want to go, Papa. Not sure what there is to say."

"You'll regret it later if you don't."

"Did you?"

"Talk to her? Yes, briefly. There wasn't much to say that hadn't already been said. I understand why she's leaving, and I can deal with it. It's been a long time coming and now that it's here … " he shrugs, "it's actually something of a relief. But, chica, I'm not her daughter."

I draw small circles with the tip of my boot. "All right, I'll go. For you." I stand on tiptoe to plant a swift kiss on his cheek.

"Gracias, mi hija." Dad turns back to the skillet. "I'd better eat this before it gets cold." He examines the eggs without making any move to scoop them onto his plate.

I head for the door, pausing before I step into the hall. I catch Dad still staring at the skillet. "You're really okay?"

"Sure," he replies, with a smile. A sad smile, but still … "It's just going to be different, you know?"

"New," I tell him. "It's going to be new. A brand new life."

This time I receive a real smile.

***

My steps slow as I approach the lab. I know my mother's disappointed in my decision to remain on Eco. Just like I'm hurt by her decision to leave—especially after I said I wouldn't accompany her.

Mom's standing in the middle of the room, the filtered light creating a nimbus about her golden hair. All her things have been cleared away, and I realize she's already moved her belongings to the Augusta Ada and only returned to speak with me.

To tell me goodbye.

"Still time to change your mind," she says, as I walk toward her.

A few feet separate us. Soon it will be millions upon millions of miles. Facing her, it occurs to me how young she looks. She has many years ahead of her—plenty of time to rebuild her life, to recreate herself. To become whatever it is she wants to be.

I straighten to my full height and meet her determined gaze. "I'm staying—for now. I have things I need to do before I can think of leaving."

"And I'm leaving—for now." Her lovely lips curve into a smile. "I won't say forever, because that's not how things work. Hope you've learned that."

"I have. One thing you've taught me."

The smile leaves her eyes. "A good lesson. Nothing is forever, my dear. Change and adapt if you want to survive."

"And if I want to do more than that?"

My mother closes the gap between us in two strides. "Then you must find what matters to you and pursue it, whatever the obstacles." She presses her cool hand against my cheek. "You must know yourself and what you want."

I gaze into her hazel eyes. They reflect, as always, her fierce will, but something else as well. It might be pride. It might even be love.

"That's my plan." I capture her falling hand and close my fingers around it. "I hope you find that, Mama, for yourself. With Captain Patel, traveling, or whatever."

She tilts her head and examines me, her eyes bright and beautiful as those of Eco's lizards. "I will try. I've never really known exactly what I wanted, you see, so that's the first step." She swings our clasped hands. "Don't be shocked if I don't stay with Connor, though. Not really sure about that yet. Early days."

I think about Raid and Dace. "I won't be shocked. You will follow through on divorcing Dad, I hope? Not right to keep him hanging on."

"I will." She pulls her hand from mine and crosses her arms across her chest. "When did you become so grown-up? I expected you to fight to keep us together."

"When you weren't looking." Despite my best intentions, I can't resist a little jab.

A sound suspiciously like a chuckle escapes her lips. "Oh, you'll do just fine, Ann." Her bright expression fades. "Will you answer, if I call you?"

"Of course," I say. "If you're paying."

She laughs out loud and pulls me into an unexpected embrace. "Ann Cooper Solano, you will definitely be just fine."

I hug her and step back, out of her arms. "Wrong name if you're planning to holo me, Mom. It's Anna-Maria Solano."

She looks me up and down. "Very well." As she walks past me, heading for the door, she allows her fingers to graze my bare arm. "Are you coming to see us off?"

"No. I already said goodbye to Dace. And I guess this is our goodbye."

Mom pauses in the doorway. "A temporary farewell. I expect to meet up with you soon, my dear, in space or elsewhere."

"Maybe on Earth, if Emie and I achieve our goals."

"Now that is something I would happily put credits on," says my mother. She leaves the room without looking back.

A temporary farewell. Just like my goodbye to Dace. Because, if I've learned anything from my very difficult, very brilliant mother, it's that you can never predict what the next moment might bring.

***

Grandmother is in the greenhouse. I see her dark head moving behind a screen of tangled sweet potato vines.

"The ship just took off," I call out as I make way down the aisle to her side.

"I heard it. Not deaf yet." She continues clipping tendrils of vine to the metal grid.

"Mom's gone."

"And your friend?" Grandmother looks over at me, her dark eyes glittering like the silver-flecked stone of the cavern.

"Yes, but it's not forever. I mean, for either of them. I'll see them again."

"Of course." Grandmother straightens, pressing her fist into the small of her back. "There'll come a day when I can't do this anymore. You planning to stick around to help out, or should I be training someone else?"

I want to lie, but know there's no point. "You might want to find a few additional kids to train. I'll be here for a few years yet, but I don't know about after that."

"Going to study at the virtual u, are you?"

"Yes. General stuff, and then Law. If I can."

Grandmother looks me up and down. "You can do anything

you put your mind to, I expect. So that's that." A slow smile spreads across her face. "I figured you'd come to it eventually. The thing you'd put all your heart and soul into. Knew it wouldn't be this." She waves one hand, indicating the rows of plants.

"It is very important, what you do."

"Sure, but it isn't for you. Bien. We all have our own paths."

I fiddle with the leaves on one of the vines. "Like Mom. She has her own path too."

"Took her awhile to decide. Best if you don't do that, nieta. Or at least, don't involve too many other people until you're sure."

That brings up the other thing on my mind. "Abuelita," I say, leaning against one of the building supports in what I hope is a nonchalant pose, "how do you know if you're sure? Like in relationships, for instance."

Grandmother wipes her hands on her work apron before turning to face me. "Like whether you should be dating Raid or that Keeling boy, you mean?"

There's no fooling her. I don't know why I even try. "Yes. I like them both, you see. I don't know what to do about that."

"Why do you have to do anything?"

"Well, I mean—sometimes I think I want to be with Raid, but then when I'm with Dace ... "

Grandmother moves close to me, until we're standing toe-to-toe. "Anna-Maria, how old are you?"

"Seventeen. You know that."

A little smile plays about her lips. "Yes, seventeen. Which means you have so much time to figure all this out. So much time. Years and years." She takes hold of one of my hands. "As

long as you're honest and don't make prom
why do you have to choose?"

"I don't know. I thought … " I stare at ɪ

Grandmother tips up my chin with one finger, forcing ....
look into her eyes. "You are so young, nieta. With so much yet to
learn, to experience. Now is not the time to decide. Now is the
time to discover."

I stare at her as those words register and I realize—as usual—
she's right. I don't have to choose now. I can love more than one
person, as long as I don't promise them things like forever. If I'm
fair. If I always tell them the truth.

If I'm willing to lose them if they find their "forever" before
I'm ready to choose mine.

"Any more work that needs doing around here?" I push
myself away from the support and roll up my sleeves.

Grandmother's face expresses her approval better than anyone
else's words. "There's always work that needs doing around here.
Come on, let's get to it. No time like the present."

CHAPTER TWENTY-FIVE

Raid is waiting with two solar bikes when I close up the greenhouse.

"We going somewhere?" I consider the dirt caked under my fingernails. I'm sure I look a mess—sweaty and smudged with nutrient fluid mixed with earth, my hair springing free of my braid and curling around my face.

It doesn't matter, though. This is me.

And this is Raid, who still sports a greenish discoloration around one temple and eye. "Thought we might head out to check on the Selk," he says, tossing me a helmet. "Told you I found a new entrance to the cavern system. Much easier access."

"Yes, you told me." I grab one of the bikes. "I was actually going to ask about that. But do we have time to get there and back before dark and still spend time with the Selk?"

Climbing astride the bike, Raid eyes me with interest. "If we put on some speed."

"A race?" I fasten my helmet, leaving the visor up. Thinking of racing reminds me of Dace and how he's rocketing away from Eco on the Augusta Ada. "Are you up for that?"

"Are you kidding?" Race flashes a grin. "Now, to make it more fun, how 'bout a little wager?"

"What kind?" I narrow my eyes.

"Oh, nothing bad." Raid pops on his helmet and adjusts the strap. "Winner just gets to ask one favor, that's all. That *must* be granted," he adds, flipping down his visor and taking off.

I rev my engine and speed after him. The problem is he knows the way and I don't. So of course he's bound to win.

Just like he planned.

After we race over the hard, dusty ground for some time, my bike almost parallel to his, he pulls away in a wide spin, stopping by a circle of low rocks. "We're here," he says, after yanking off his helmet. "And I won."

"Hardly fair and square." I dismount and prop my bike with the kickstand. Hanging my helmet over the handlebars, I look around but see nothing that appears to be the entrance to a cave. "Where the hell are we? There're no rock hills nearby."

Raid smiles and motions for me to move closer to him. I walk forward until he throws out an arm to halt my progress.

"Optical illusion," he says. "We've been traveling uphill so slowly, you didn't notice the incline." He takes my hand and walks me forward a few steps.

I'm staring down into an open well, similar to the one Dace and I found. This one is wider, with a gently inclined path that leads to a vegetation-covered pool.

"See that shadow?" Raid leads me down the path, still holding my hand. "That's the entrance to another underground lake. Just beyond the curve of the passage."

As we make our way down, I note the varied types of vegetation growing along the edge of the pool. More research for Dace. Or maybe, for my grandmother. I wonder if I can convince her to venture out into the wilderness to examine these plants.

"This way," says Raid, pulling me into the darkness of the passageway.

He's prepared, switching on a solar light he brought along. We only have to walk a few paces in the dark, though, before we step into a cavern.

This one boasts a wide, perfectly round skylight that rises above the lake like a dome. It must open directly to the surface.

"Have to be careful in the future." Raid voices the thought running through my head. "Now we know some openings aren't marked by any rock piles."

"Good idea." I reply automatically, distracted by the sheer size of this cavern and the width of the lake it encloses. It's so large that I have to readjust my thinking. This is a lake—the other caves we've visited hold ponds. Attached to one side wall, a spur of rock juts into the middle of the lake like a stone finger. Several clusters of Selk lounge on this rock peninsula, while others frolic in the water.

"Come swim with me." Raid holds out his hands.

"What about the wager?"

"This is it. This is what I want." Raid grins. "What'd you think I'd ask for?"

I shake my head. "Not sure." Of course, I thought he'd demand a kiss, at the very least. Swimming with the Selk never crossed my mind.

"You have a very dirty mind, Ann. Now—strip."

I spare one thought for what I'm wearing under my jeans and jacket: a dark blue T-shirt and black underpants. I suppose that will do. I sit on a nearby rock ledge to pull off my boots and socks.

"Slow-poke." Raid, already stripped down to his boxers and a T-shirt, darts over and reaches for my legs. "We don't have all day," he says, yanking off my jeans.

"Wait up," I say, but Raid has already dashed to the lake and slid into its clear water. I walk to the edge and stare down, calculating the depth. Good enough.

Before Raid realizes what I'm doing, I jump in, grabbing my knees to my chest to create a great splash.

"Hey!" He sputters as I surface and swim up to face him. "Where'd you learn that?"

"From those old films my other grandmother brought to Eco. It's called a cannonball, by the way."

"Good term for it." Raid reaches for me.

Hah, I see his game. Now he'll try to kiss me.

But no. "Race you to those rocks," he says, and takes off, all flashing arms and kicking legs.

I chase after him and we reach the rock peninsula at the same time. Clinging to an outcropping of stone, we turn to each other, breathing hard.

We lean in at the same moment. This kiss tastes tangy, like the mineral-laced water lapping silkily about us. Raid uses his free hand to pull me closer. Soaked as we are, our clothing molds to us, and I feel we're pressed skin upon skin all along the length of our bodies. Raid groans softly, and I wrap my buoyant legs, light as flower petals, around his waist.

"Dangerous," he whispers in my ear.

At that moment, something butts against my back. I pull away from Raid and look over my shoulder—into the face of one of the Selk.

"Oh, hell," says Raid, with a strangled laugh. "Chaperones."

Several more Selk swim up, surrounding us in a wide arc. Their bright brown eyes survey us with comical solemnity.

Friends. Above.

I'm prepared for the mental onslaught now. I nod and send my own greeting forward. *Yes, friends. Humans. From above.*

The Selk use their tails to propel themselves backward, still keeping their eyes fixed on us.

Play.

I cast a surprised glance at Raid. "Did you hear that? They said … "

"Play," Raid finishes. He stares at me, his mouth twitching.

I giggle. "Play. They want to play."

"So—you up for it?"

I nod and we both swim out into the circle of Selk.

We play—diving and gliding underwater, swimming in circles and figure eights as the Selk leap and spin around us. After a while the Selk drift away, some scrambling onto the rock promontory to rest, and some gliding off toward the other side of the lake.

Raid and I swim to the shore. Pulling ourselves onto the

bank, we sit in silence for some time, holding hands as we watch the water creatures move about the lake.

When we rise to our feet I stride over to my other clothes, discarded in a darker spot of the cavern. I slip on my T-shirt, then hop as I tug the jeans up each leg.

Raid watches this procedure, amusement sparkling in his dark eyes. "I'd be glad to help, you know."

"I can do it," I say, and slip and fall on my butt.

Raid rushes to me, but I wave him away. "I'm fine. Just … " I press my hand against the stone floor of the cavern to push myself up. Something digs into my palm. "Mierda, what's this? Smooth for a rock." My fingers close over the object.

Raid extends his hand. "A crystal or something?"

"Maybe. Help me up."

Raid pulls me to my feet with one hand. I keep my fingers clenched around the object in my other palm. We walk closer to the lake, where the light is brighter. Standing close to Raid's side, I uncurl my fingers.

In my palm lies a small, perfectly formed image of one of the Selk. A tiny sculpture, created from some gleaming white metal I can't identify.

Raid and I look at each other. "Where did that … ?" he says, then falls silent and just strokes the little statue with the tip of one finger. "It's beautiful."

"Yes." I look out over the lake. A small cluster of Selk glide near the shore. They bob in the water, watching us.

I hold out my palm. The rays falling from the skylight touch the sculpture, making it glitter like a star. I close my eyes for a moment to concentrate my thoughts. *Us? Also us?*

There's a flurry in the water. I open my eyes as the Selk draw closer, right to the edge of the lake. Their dark eyes fasten on the object shining in my palm.

The word that rings through my brain is so unexpected I almost drop the tiny sculpture. Instead, I pocket it and take Raid's hand. Without another word we pull on our socks and shoes, gather up our jackets, and leave the cavern. Clinging to one another, we retrace our steps and quickly make our way to the solar bikes.

Raid grabs his helmet from his bike's handlebars. "We should head back. It's getting late. Don't want to be caught out in the dark." He gazes out over the barren landscape, his helmet dangling by its strap from his fingers.

"Right. Got a lot to do tomorrow. I need to sign up for my virtual u courses and Emie wants me to help her draft some petitions for the 'sphere, and there's our regular work, of course, and … "

"Ann," Raid turns to me, his eyes searching my face. "Did you hear it? Did you hear what they said?"

I swallow hard. "I heard something. But it's loco."

Raid puts his arm around my shoulders and pulls me close. "I heard one word."

We stare out over the landscape. The quiet, empty, dust-over-stone world of Eco. Our birth planet. Our home.

Them, the Selk had said, when I asked who'd created the beautiful object in my pocket. Not *Us.*

Them.

ACKNOWLEDGEMENTS

I would like to express my sincere gratitude to the following people for their support and assistance in the creation of FACSIMILE:

My dedicated and innovative publisher – Georgia McBride and the entire team at Month9Books.

My agency – Literary Counsel. Special thanks to Fran Black.

My wonderful critique partners – Lindsey Duga, Steve Katzen, and Richard Pearson.

My fantastic family, especially my husband, Kevin Weavil.

All the authors of speculative fiction who have enchanted, enthralled, educated, and entertained me over the years. They opened my mind to worlds of wonder when I was a child, and have continued to do so throughout my life. Thanks, fellow authors, for teaching me to always consider "What if?"

VICKI L. WEAVIL

Vicki Lemp Weavil was raised in a farming community in Virginia, where her life was shaped by a wonderful family, the culture of the Blue Ridge Mountains, and an obsession with reading. Since obtaining her undergraduate degree in Theatre from the University of Virginia, she's gone on to acquire two masters degrees, living in places as diverse as New York City and rural North Carolina. She's currently the library director for a performing an visual arts university. Vicki loves good writing in any genre, and has been known to read seven books in as many days. She enjoys travel, gardening, and the arts. Vicki lives in North Carolina with her husband, son, and some very spoiled cats.

OTHER MONTH9BOOKS TITLES YOU MIGHT LIKE

CROWN OF ICE
LIFE, A.D.
VESSEL
FIRE IN THE WOODS

Find more awesome Teen books at http://www.Month9Books.com

Connect with Month9Books online:
Facebook: www.Facebook.com/Month9Books
Twitter: https://twitter.com/Month9Books
You Tube: www.youtube.com/user/Month9Books
Blog: www.month9booksblog.com
Instagram: https://instagram.com/month9books
Request review copies via publicity@month9books.com

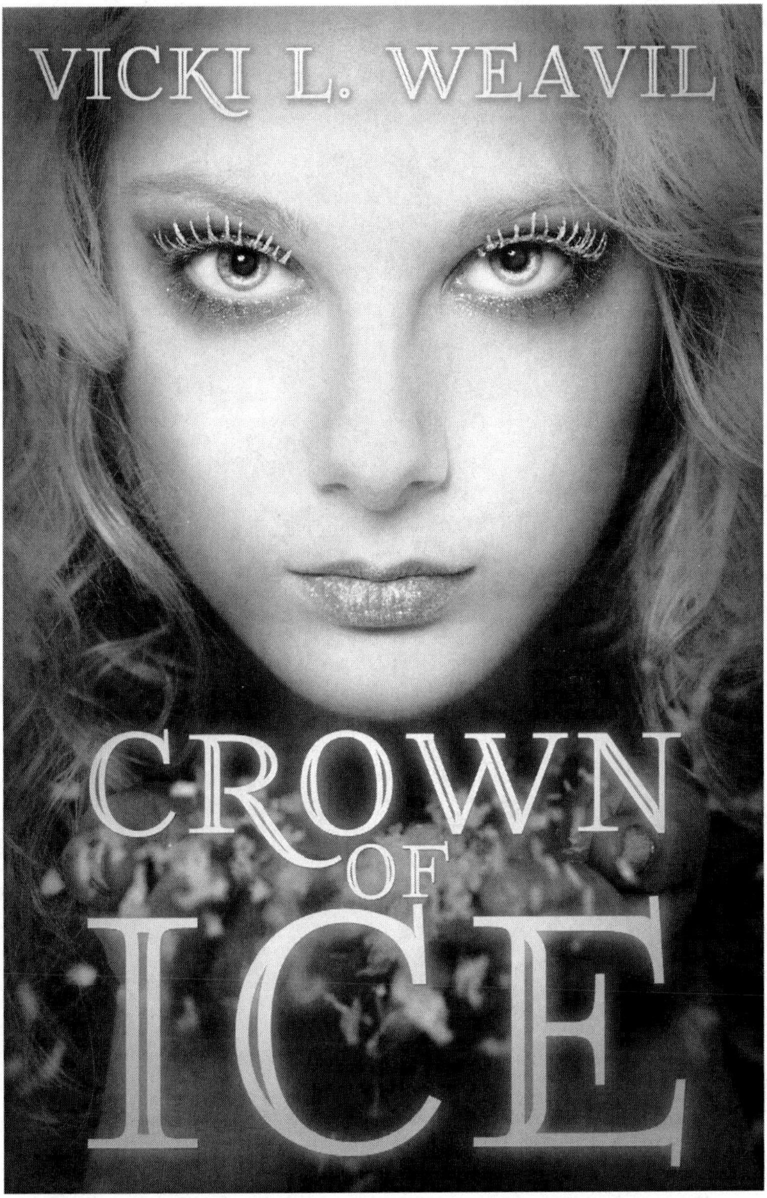
VICKI L. WEAVIL
CROWN
OF
ICE

LIFE, A.D.
Life, After. Dez.

MICHELLE E. REED

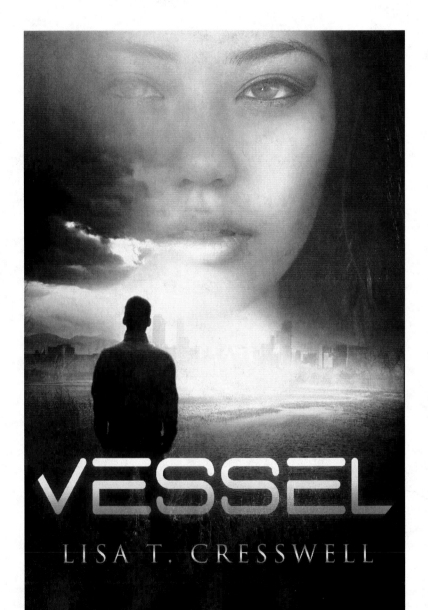

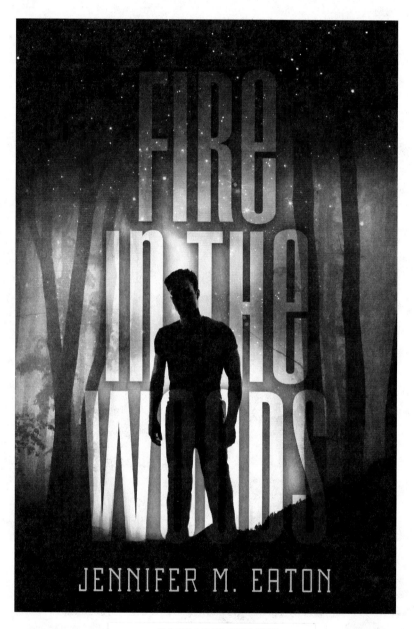

FIRE IN THE WOODS

JENNIFER M. EATON